Would Adrianna's love survive this trial by fire?

Face perspiring, cheeks flaming, Adrianna felt suddenly cold inside, hollow. "Your fundamentals—your principles—" she choked. "Are they more important than losing the *Mignonne* to Green?"

"Of course. Our defeats are merely punctuation, commas in God's plan for us. Let Green have his money and power. What we have is . . ."

Adrianna fled.

Flinging herself upon her bed, she wept her misery. How Foy and his family must hate her! Everything was all her fault!

Persistent knocking at her cabin door penetrated her sobs. Foy and Lily called, pleaded. She would not let them in.

Darkness fell. Everything seemed lost.

JACQUELYN COOK is a veteran inspirational romance author whose extensive research brings alive the gracious living of the people of Eufaula, Alabama, during the late 1800s. *River of Fire* is the third book in a trilogy of novels that includes *The River Between* and *The Wind Along the River*.

River of Fire

Jacquelyn Cook

Heartsong Presents

For
Mama and Daddy
Carolyn and Arlene

ISBN 1-55748-334-5

RIVER OF FIRE

PRINTED IN U.S.A.

one

Sunlight kindled red and gold flames in the curls cascading down Adrianna's back as she strolled along Eufaula Street, happily noting that store windows contained merchandise from around the world now that the war was over. She paused to admire millinery for the fall of 1874 in the window of Stern's Temple of Fashion.

Suddenly she realized the street was quiet, deserted. Shops were closed. Did everyone in Alabama take a nap after the noon meal?

She swallowed nervously. She had noticed soldiers in the hotel. Now there was no one in sight, and she had completely lost direction.

Out of the corner of her eye, she glimpsed a lean young man moving toward her with hard-muscled strides. His fine nose and chin and his confident carriage bore the mark of a gentleman, even though the cut of his waistcoat was outdated. As he neared, Adrianna looked quickly away.

Twirling her lace-trimmed parasol over her shoulder, Adrianna stepped along Hart's Block. The feel of eyes upon her back made her shiver. Even though she practiced ignoring people who stared at her brilliant hair, especially against her bottle green street costume, she could not resist a peep at the vigorous man.

He had broken into a lope. Her tense frown smoothed into a tender smile as she saw within the man the image of a small boy, arms and legs flapping.

"Wait!" he shouted as he neared her. "You must—come

with me—before . . ."

Snapping her head away from him, she quickened her pace. His strong hand grasped her shoulder.

"Please," he said, panting. "Listen, ma'am. I'd never hurt you. You must let me take you back to your hotel. You're walking to the polling place, and—"

"Certainly not, sir," she said icily. "We have not been introduced."

For a moment he stared in consternation, then a slow smile filled his lean face. Doffing his high silk hat, he bowed low and intoned, "May I present Foy Edwards, Esquire."

Giggling in spite of herself, she responded, "Hello, I'm Adrianna Atherton."

Clapping his hat back on his head, he grasped her elbow. "That's done. Now come on," he said urgently and headed her down the empty street in the opposite direction.

Shrill piping and menacing drumbeats shattered the stillness. An angry roar of voices clashed against the music. Wrenching around, Adrianna saw the street filling with armed men.

She shrieked, and her knees buckled.

"Don't play Lot's wife. Come on!"

His arm shot around her trim waist. As he half-carried her, she felt the hard outline of a pistol against her ribs. Behind them rang the shouts of the mob.

"Who?" she gasped. "What?"

"That's the Radical Party, and—" Scuffling sounds behind them increased his pace. "Run!"

A shot echoed and reechoed against the brick buildings. For one long moment there was deathly silence. Then hundreds of shots rained down from the upper floors of the storehouses.

"That's the Democrats. We're 'bout to the hotel. Oh, good

grannies!" He jerked her to a stop.

Adrianna blinked at a wall of blue-coated soldiers.

"And that's the Federal Occupation Army!" He spat out the words.

Her parasol dropped with a clatter as they darted into an alley. Running blindly, she had begun to think she could go no farther when he stopped abruptly, leaped astride a horse, and swung her up behind him. Sitting sidesaddle as they galloped away, Adrianna held tightly to the back of her rescuer with one hand and clutched her hat with the other.

When they reached a quiet street lined with China trees, he slowed the sorrel to a trot. Clucking to the horse, he turned in at a gate and rode up a drive past huge red cedars.

Adrianna stared at the tremendous house spreading before her. Wildly overgrown shrubs screened the verandah. Her eyes moved up to the balcony on the second story and higher still to the glassed belvedere and widow's walk which crowned the roof.

"Welcome to Barbour Hall," he said as he dismounted. Lifting her from the sorrel's back, he observed, "You're a young lady of contradictions. Your hair looks like maple leaves in autumn, yet your perfume..." He sniffed experimentally. "Ah, the first breath of spring." He beamed down at her as he reluctantly dropped his hands and stepped away.

"It's French hyacinths." She swallowed and her blue-green eyes gazed wonderingly at him.

He cleared his throat, turned toward the house, and frowned.

Watching his brows knit together as he looked from her to the house, Adrianna could tell he was realizing for the first time how shabby it had become. She wondered why such a magnificent mansion had been neglected. If her grandfather's wealth had diminished since the war, she had not realized it.

Looking at his home, the serious young man said ruefully, "My sister used to say she looked like a hoop-skirted belle dressed for a ball, but now she's a dowdy old dowager."

"Your sister?" She pressed one finger to her lips to suppress a laugh.

"No," he said, chuckling. "She's grown more beautiful with maturity. I meant the house."

"Well." She pursed her lips. "Hoop skirts are out of style." She saw what he meant about the delicately trimmed, spreading porch. "But a house would look funny with a bustle." She laughed delightedly at the thought, then said more seriously, "Pruning the shrubs and painting the house would work wonders."

"I hadn't noticed how badly she'd gone down since Mama died three years ago." He removed his hat and pushed back thick hair. "I really must get some work done on her, but I haven't been able—I can't ask you in."

"Oh, that's all right. I don't mind a little dirt." She started up the steps.

"No." His voice was a deep rumble. "I'm a bachelor. It wouldn't be proper for you to go in unchaperoned."

Adrianna pursed her lips and said, "That's old-fashioned. I can certainly trust the man who saved my life."

"No." The determined set of his chin stopped her mid-step. "I would not sully your reputation. Come. We'll sit in the summerhouse until it's safe to take you to the hotel."

Meekly following along the boxwood-bordered path, she broke the silence. "Seriously, I do thank you for coming to my aid. It's a good thing you happened along."

"I didn't just happen along." He looked down at her. "I was waiting in an upstairs window—no, not for you." He grinned at her mock surprise. "We were expecting trouble. That mob was marching through the county, voting at every precinct under a different name."

"I noticed you're armed. Are you a law officer?"

"No. The marshals and policemen had tried to intervene, but volunteer police had to be summoned." He lifted a swag of wisteria vine which drooped over the open doorway of the white-latticed gazebo.

"How do you know so much about me—that I'm at the hotel, and . . ."

With a deep chuckle he said, "I was born and bred in Eufaula, Alabama. I know all the young ladies in town—"

"I'll just bet you do!" She tossed her head coyly as she arranged her skirt on a graying wicker settee.

Ignoring the flirtatious honey in her voice, he folded his long body into a chair across from her.

"I would say . . ." He studied her in amusement. "That you're Senator Atherton's daughter."

"Granddaughter," she corrected, "but how—"

"Sixteen years ago my sister, Lily, was made ragingly jealous upon hearing that Captain Wingate was seen dancing with the most beautiful lady in Washington City," he said, laughing. "You must look exactly like your grandmother."

A smile twitched about her lips at the clever way he had complimented her without being impolitely forward.

"The lady in question doesn't take very good care of you," he continued. "You should not have been on the street unchaperoned—and not at all on election day."

"Actually," she looked down, "I came to Alabama to look after Ma-ma. Her health is failing. We arrived last evening on the train from Macon. I slipped out while my grandparents were resting for the Wingates' anniversary party, and—are you? What did you say your name was?"

He laughed and looked at her with intense brown eyes. Flustered by his probing gaze, she waited.

"Foy," he said at last. "Foy Edwards. But you can forget it again," he said, teasingly. "I plan to pretend we've never met."

"Then my grandfather . . ." She stammered, unable to breathe as she watched the change his slow smile brought to his face. "Came—came here to consult with . . ."

"With Harrison Wingate and me." He reared back in his chair, seeming imperceptibly to pull away from her. The soft intimacy of his voice became more businesslike. "Years before the war, Harrison tried to induce Congress to clear the channel of the Chattahoochee."

"That beautiful green river we crossed on the trestle coming into Eufaula?"

"Yes. It's always been dangerous. Narrow, winding, full of rocks, sandbars, snags." Foy gestured with his long arms. "And since the war—with all the sunken boats and obstructions—even a good captain like Harrison is risking his life at every turning. If we're to join the industrial boom, the river must be cleared!"

"Yes!" Her eyes sparkled as she caught his excitement. "Back East, men are becoming millionaires overnight. Factories, new machinery, marvelous inventions—oh, I love trying modern things!"

"Yes, well," Foy said seriously, "I can't approve of some of the new methods—believe in old values and principles myself." He shrugged. "But I am excited by new challenges." He leaned forward, his eyes snapping. "Harrison and I are partners in building a new steamboat. She's modern, all right, sleek, beautiful, the most luxurious appointments." He tipped the chair back with his arms behind his head and grinned at Adrianna with small-boy excitement.

"How exciting!" she exclaimed, bringing her fingertips together under her dimpled chin. "Oh, I do admire anyone who knows exactly where he's going in life. I don't know what I'm—"

Suddenly the sun, which had warmed them through the latticed roof, moved behind a cloud. A crisp breeze warned them that the November day was speeding past.

Consulting the small gold watch pinned to her bodice, Adrianna exclaimed, "Mercy! It's three o'clock. Ma-ma will be waking and—

"Yes, young lady, it's time I was taking you home." Foy flopped the chair down with a thump. "Wait here." He got up. "I'll hitch the runabout and conduct you back more properly."

"You think the riot is over?"

"Downtown, yes, but our troubles are just beginning. We've been warned of ballot stuffing at Spring Hill, eighteen miles from town."

"You'll be at the anniversary party?" Her voice was small as she tried to hide her hope.

"No," he shook his head. Worry etched his strong features. "I told Lily I couldn't make it. I'm expected to help guard the ballot box until the vote is counted. We've had a scalawag for a judge. Until we put an end to lawlessness and get a government with a strong foundation, we'll never get our world on course."

He turned at the open doorway. "I hate to miss the fun, but I'm afraid the troubles of this day are just beginning."

two

A rainbow of silks and satins spread over Adrianna's room. It was time for the party, and she still could not decide what to wear. Eyes dancing, she held up pink, then turquoise. She chose the more sophisticated.

Foy Edwards needs impressing, she thought, as she fastened her tightly laced corset. Buttoning on the corset cover and stepping into the bustle skirt with its steel hoops protruding behind her, she wavered. She did not want him to think her worldly. She shrugged into a cambric petticoat. Neither could she let him think her a child. Foy Edwards was older, fully his own man. Shivering as the turquoise taffeta rustled over her creamy shoulders, she realized that made him exciting.

Rousing herself, she hurriedly brushed her red-gold hair. Dear Ma-ma's rheumatism-twisted hands could no longer manage tiny fastenings. She would be needing Adrianna. Leaving a pouf of curls on her forehead, she combed the rest of her hair back demurely and caught it at the nape of her neck with a white silk rose.

"How about that, Mr. Edwards." She tapped the dimple in her chin and grinned impishly at her reflection.

Foy had said he was not going to the party. For a moment the thought mocked her. Of too sunny a nature to worry, Adrianna laughed. Foy Edwards would somehow arrange to get there. Humming happily she whirled out of the room on a cloud of fragrance.

When the carriage drew up to the Wingate home, Adrianna thought the house far less impressive than Barbour Hall, but as she followed her grandparents up to the wide, square-columned porch, she felt enveloped by unpretentious warmth. A tall man rushed out to meet the Washington visitors.

"It's a great pleasure to welcome you to Alabama, Senator Atherton," Harrison Wingate said in a deep voice. He shook hands with his imposing, white-haired guest. Then he bowed to kiss the gloved hand of Isadora Atherton. "And you, my lady," he said cordially. "My wife has heard so much of your beauty," he grinned, "that she feels she knows you."

Adrianna suppressed a giggle as she noticed the sidelong glance Wingate flashed at his wife. Remembering what Foy had said about Lily's jealousy, she studied her grandmother. Gray had washed Isadora's hair to a faded pink, but her voluptuous figure and beautiful bone structure still gave claim to her being a great beauty.

"We're delighted to have you," responded Lily Wingate. "Do come in out of the damp air." As she graciously welcomed her guests into the wide, central hall, Lily tossed her rich, dark hair and wrinkled her nose at her husband's teasing look.

"And this is our granddaughter, Adrianna," Samuel Pembroke Atherton said in the booming voice he used to show her off from a political platform.

"You look startlingly like your grandmother, young lady." Captain Wingate bowed elegantly over her hand.

"Why thank you, Captain Wingate," Adrianna answered with a smile in her voice. Accepting the obvious compliment, she fervently hoped she would never be as vain as her grandmother.

"I had expected you to be a child." Lily laughed uncertainly. "A friend for Mignonne, but . . ." Her voice trailed away. "What a delightful fragrance! Lighter than jasmine."

"Hyacinth." Adrianna smiled. "Are you a connoisseur of

perfumes?"

"No, no. We haven't had French perfume here lately. But I love flowers. Growing them is my favorite pastime."

Acknowledging introductions as Lily guided her about, Adrianna let her eyes drift. She quickly assessed the people to be a bit provincial. She wondered why. From what Grandfather had told her, Eufaula had been a prosperous riverboat town for fifty years. Cotton from surrounding plantations was shipped down the Chattahoochee River to the Gulf of Mexico and goods were brought back from all over the world. Planters as well as merchants had filled the town with mansions.

As her family had driven along the streets, Adrianna had been impressed by the aloof grandeur of the homes, yet as she moved through the Wingates' home, she noticed that the windows had old lace curtains instead of fashionable draperies. Most of these ladies still looked like walking mushrooms in the hoop skirts of the prewar era.

Adrianna smoothed her taffeta skirt, proudly aware that it fell stylishly straight to her toes in front. Yards of matching satin swirled tightly across her stomach and puffed elegantly behind her in a bustle.

"I understand you played a great part in saving the town from the invader's torch, Mrs. Ramsey." Senator Atherton's voice filled the room. "The cotton in the warehouses was saved too, I presume?"

Adrianna turned casually, then blinked in surprise. The heroine he addressed was a placid, middle-aged woman with white-blonde hair. She acknowledged the Senator's remark with a self-deprecating murmur. "I really didn't do that much—"

"Emma's swift action made the difference," interrupted a man whose devoted smile indicated that he must be her husband. "We were fortunate that her warning saved Eufaula from being burned and looted as so many parts of Alabama and your state of Georgia were, sir."

Emma Ramsey smiled with contentment as the jovial man squeezed her shoulder. "We were lucky that General Grierson was a gentleman," she said in a quiet voice, "and waited for proof that the armistice had been signed."

Jonathan Ramsey raked his fingers through thick, iron-gray curls. "In answer to your other question, sir, Grierson was not quite as kind as we first thought. On his march through Alabama, he saw three hundred thousand bales of cotton which he was good enough *not* to destroy. " He laughed bitterly, but the crinkles around his eyes showed his unflagging humor. "When the war was over, however, Grierson jumped on our cotton like a duck on a June bug. He said he was determined to break the spirit of the town's aristocrats and their finances as well."

"We tried to help young Foy," interjected Harrison Wingate. Adrianna gave her full attention.

"Help get his father's Cotton Exchange on its feet," he explained. "Foy had served two years in the Confederate Navy and like all leading southern men, was accused of treason and disfranchised. Ironically, some of us were given back the right to vote sooner than Foy because he held more than $20,000 in taxable property—held it briefly, that is. Grierson and the Federal Government confiscated every bale of his cotton."

Tears stung Adrianna's eyes as sympathetic understanding of the decay of Barbour Hall flooded through her. She looked toward the still-empty hallway. Their meeting no doubt had meant nothing to him, but she could think of no one but Foy Edwards.

Munching a tangy shrimp mousse offered to her by a butler, Adrianna turned back to the conversation. Harrison Wingate was explaining how his steamboat, *Wave*, had been deliberately sunk across the Chattahoochee to block the advance of the enemy.

Behind her ivory fan, Adrianna's cheeks blazed as she listened to the Captain explain how he and Foy Edwards were building a new steamboat while fighting to get the river cleared. She had misjudged these people as behind the times. Now she listened with growing admiration for the spirit with which they endeavored to rebuild their lives. She wished she had not flaunted her expensive dress direct from the Paris haute couture salon of Charles Frederick Worth.

Over her fan, Adrianna peered across the parlor to the doorway. She sniffed disgustedly. Foy was not coming.

Solicitously, she turned to help Mama with the thin china teacup which shook in her swollen fingers. Behind them raged a heated discussion about unbearable tax burdens. In some places, they had been increased by 500 percent. Talk of taxes meant little until she heard her grandfather's question.

"I say, Ramsey, don't you own a plantation in Georgia?"

"I did," he replied heatedly. "In Bulloch County. Everything at Magnolia Springs was completely destroyed during Sherman's ravaging march. The last I heard, it was being held for taxes. As if taxes had not been raised enough, I can only redeem my plantation by paying double the tax!"

Emma explained softly to Isadora and Adrianna, "His six-year-old daughter, Elizabeth, was there at the time. We could never find a trace of what happened to her."

Having been a child at home with her mother in Madison, Georgia, a town uniquely spared by General Sherman, Adrianna had thought little about the War Between the

States in which more than half a million men had died and another half million had been wounded. She had never realized that these last few years of Reconstruction had been far worse for the South than war.

Again her eyes drifted to the door. She saw that someone else was watching. Across the hall in the music room stood a petite beauty with hair as black and shining as a bird's wing. Attired in glowing pink velvet draped in a more fashionable polonaise, the girl looked like a French porcelain doll. Beneath flirtatious bangs, her snapping dark eyes guarded the door.

"We had hoped, Senator Atherton, that perhaps," Harrison Wingate's quiet voice demanded attention. "Perhaps, since Georgia has had three years with conservative government re-established—and since honest voters have returned you and you've finally been reseated in the Senate—" Everyone in the room turned toward him as his voice shook with emotion. "If we don't have an honest election this time, maybe you could start a congressional investigation." Harrison turned his hands eloquently. "Being under a Federal Army of Occupation is not the bitterest pill, nor even having our elected officials controlled by northerners come South with all their worldly goods in small bags made of carpet. The worst problems are from our corrupt city court judge, Elias Keils. Our crooked government is enriching a few and giving no protection to life and property. We fear for the safety of our families!"

Lily turned to Adrianna and her grandmother. "I do apologize, ladies, for having the party in the midst of a furor. I guess I'm just too sentimental. Our wedding day, November 3, 1858, was so special that I wanted to have our anniversary party today even though it was election Tuesday."

"That's quite all right, my dear." Isadora Atherton smiled

regally. "We napped. We slept right through the disturbance."

Adrianna felt a blush rising and fanned rapidly. The quick calculation that the Wingates had been married for sixteen years surprised her. From the moment she had stepped into their home, she had felt their love.

The house of her childhood had been an echoing emptiness of chilly silences. Her parents had finally separated, and she had been shunted around among them and her grandparents.

Wistfully, Adrianna watched the tall, quiet man smile across the parlor into the lively eyes of his vivacious wife as if they were newlyweds. Folding her fan in her lap, Adrianna let her longing eyes assess them openly. Even as their harmony enveloped their guests, they seemed set apart by a special closeness. Adrianna's full lips quivered with desire to share that kind of oneness with someone special.

Laughter rippled around her. Adrianna shook herself and tried to listen to Jonathan Ramsey joke about the riot.

"And old Lige said that when the shooting started he eased up close to E.M. Bounds. 'I figered,' " Jonathan mimicked, " 'if they was any man in town the Lord would take care of it'ud be the Rev. Mr. Bounds.' "

Chuckles broke off as his story was interrupted by a commotion in the entrance hall. The door burst open. A disheveled man entered and shouted the news: "There's been trouble at Old Spring Hill. The bullets found their mark in an innocent young man. He lies dying!"

Adrianna stiffened in horror as she saw Lily fling her hand to her throat and mouth the silent word, "Foy."

three

"Foy!" Adrianna inhaled his name. Wingate calmly moved through the room. Clapping his hand upon the man's shoulder, he gave a quiet command. "Get hold of yourself, Samuel. Slowly now. Who's wounded? What happened?"

"The boy. Not his father." Samuel shook with emotion. "Little Willie Keils."

Adrianna sank back against the settee, thankful that it had not been Foy. Taking a bracing sip of tea, she listened to the man's tale.

"The polls closed at five o'clock. Foy and I and several others were guarding—trying to help the Spring Hill folks keep the peace. Old Judge Keils had gone out there—"

"Yes." Harrison stopped the flow of details. "Just tell us what happened."

"Keils barred the door. The managers began counting the ballots. Suddenly a group of men made a rush, firing double-barreled shotguns as they ran. A clerk unlocked the door. They rushed in—knocked out the lamp. It was black as midnight. Shots were flying. I could've hit Foy myself."

"What?" Harrison shook him. "Foy's hurt?"

"Just nicked. He's all right. Doc Weedon's patching him up."

A collective sigh released.

"It was Keils they were after. Some say little Willie threw himself in front of his father. It was easy to mistake a boy for such a slightly built man in the dark. Four bullets rained into the child. When the lamp was lit, the ballots were burning. Elias

Keils was cowering in a corner with some of the mob ready to hang him. He begged Mr. Wallace as a lodge brother to save him. They respected Mr. Wallace—him and the pistols he held in each hand."

Samuel gulped another breath. Seeing Harrison's meaningful glare, he finished his story. "Bad as his lodge brothers hated his crookedness, they saved Keils by escorting him to jail. But I'm afraid little Willie's dying."

Adrianna had not heard the door open again, but suddenly there stood Foy. His left arm rested in a sling. Rising quickly, she started toward him.

The petite brunette who had also been watching stepped swiftly from the music room. She softly kissed Foy's cheek.

With an aching sigh, Adrianna drew behind a fern stand and watched miserably. No wonder he knew about French perfume.

"I'm fine, I'm fine!" Foy's deep voice assured Lily, who hurried to him and brushed his thick hair from his pale face with a trembling hand. "It's just a scratch. Really," he said, embarrassed.

Adrianna could read loving concern on the plain face of Emma Ramsey. So all the women love him, she thought. Adrianna wished she could touch his lean cheeks, smooth his furrowed brow. Surprised at this longing, she chided herself that Foy surely charmed every woman who met him. Adrianna leaned forward to catch Foy's words.

"Let's not disrupt your party, Lily," he said, forcing a smile. "Introduce me to your guests."

Adrianna could feel her cheeks betraying her as he crossed the parlor.

"I say, this must be the young man I've been hearing such good things about!" Her grandfather's voice resounded in Adrianna's ears as he stepped in front of her with his hand outstretched. "Distinguished career in the navy, I understand."

Foy shook the proffered hand and replied sardonically, "I'm afraid my most memorable act was striking the match to burn our gunboat, *Chattahoochee*, before the enemy could take her. But I did gain a love for the river," he continued earnestly. "We appreciate your coming, sir. We have great plans." His voice rose with enthusiasm. "We hope you'll have time to see the steamboat we're building. She's a real beauty!"

Foy grinned at his own exuberance. "There's a promise of a good cotton crop this year, and if you can send us engineers to help clear the channel, this section of Georgia, Alabama, and Florida can make a comeback."

Adrianna struggled to regain her poise as her grandfather discussed the situation with Foy. At long last he turned to Isadora, who preened as the young man bowed before her.

"It's a great pleasure to meet you, Mrs. Atherton." Foy brushed a polite kiss over her majestically extended hand. "Word of your great beauty preceded you."

When Foy finally was presented to her, Adrianna managed to gaze disinterestedly at him.

"How delightful to meet you, Miss Atherton." His deep voice was coolly formal, but he pressed a genuine kiss upon her hand. His eyes twinkled merrily at her discomfort. With a sly wink, he asked, "Did I hear that you are a horsewoman?"

Adrianna's cheeks twitched as she tried to keep from laughing.

Foy turned and bowed again to Isadora. "Would you trust a stranger and accord me the honor of escorting your grand-daughter on a ride about our fair city tomorrow afternoon?"

"I'd love to!" Adrianna blurted. Her high spirits bubbled as Isadora considered, then nodded. Meeting his warm gaze, Adrianna said mischievously, "I find staying in a hotel room quite confining." A giggle escaped and she looked away to control her mirth. The black-haired beauty stood clingingly behind Foy.

Realizing she had appeared anxious, Adrianna amended, "Perhaps another time." Biting her lip, she hesitated. "Your arm?"

The girl nudged Foy. Adrianna frowned, thinking her far too young for him.

"A scratch," he said, shrugging. "Shall I call for you at three?" He looked down at the girl who was pinching him. "Have you met Mignonne?"

"No," she replied coolly.

"Minnie, may I present Miss Adrianna Atherton."

"It's so exciting to meet you, Miss Atherton," she said, stretching her words into floating syllables like molasses sliding over a stack of hotcakes. "Living in Washington must be just marvelous."

Adrianna's jealousy melted slightly at the sincere admiration in the younger girl's manner. But she was not pleased when dinner was announced and she was seated with Mignonne far down the table from Foy and her grandfather. Making the best of it, she chatted pleasantly and answered the girl's endless questions.

Mignonne kept staring at her hair. "Whatever do you put on your hair to give it that stunning color?"

"Nothing!" Adrianna retorted. "Why would anyone want to dye their hair flaming red?"

Mignonne's dark eyes filled with tears. "I didn't mean to be rude, ma'am."

Adrianna laughed lightly and patted the girl's hand. "That's all right. I'm sorry I sounded annoyed. It's just that I'm asked that so much! I should be used to it by now." She took a bite of candied sweet potatoes. "This is certainly a delicious meal."

She tried her best to be nice to Mignonne, but her attention kept drifting to Foy. She caught only snatches of conversation as he told the Senator how he had drawn a detailed map of the river showing where hulls of sunken boats prevented passage. The men planned a morning meeting at the river to discuss securing an appropriation from Congress to clear the channel of the Chattahoochee, and the evening came to an end.

Adrianna donned her smartly tailored, brown riding habit early and prowled the hotel suite nervously. Gray mists had shrouded the morning with foreboding. She feared that Mama would not allow her to go out on horseback if the weather did not clear.

A brisk knock sent her scurrying across the room. She threw open the door with a wide, welcoming smile.

There stood Mignonne.

"I hope," Foy said, peeping around the plume of Mignonne's riding hat, "that we haven't kept you waiting. Harrison, Senator Atherton, and I had so much business. Good afternoon, Mrs. Atherton. You're feeling well, I trust?"

Turning aside to hide her disappointment, Adrianna had no need for words.

Isadora swept forward from the adjoining bedroom.

"Yes, thank you," she cooed as she commandingly extended her hand for him to kiss. "I find the atmosphere of your fair city as pure as mountain air." Her voice and intimate smile made it seem he had created it especially for her.

Putting on her narrow-brimmed hat and kid gloves, Adrianna watched her grandmother. Isadora had dressed in a becoming afternoon frock which matched her hair. For the first time, Adrianna suspected that Ma-ma used dye. Her artifice seemed lost upon Foy. Responding seriously, he explained he had brought Mignonne so that Mrs. Atherton need not worry they would be unchaperoned. He assured her that the disturbance seemed over for the time being.

Adrianna swallowed her resentment. Foy's apparent attraction had fooled her. His feeling toward her had been as shallow as everyone else's in her young life. The warm camaraderie between Foy and Mignonne spoke with swift eloquence that they cared about each other. Her cheeks pale, her green eyes wistful, Adrianna morosely followed them into a day which remained as gray as her mood.

Foy bowed elaborately as he helped them mount their horses. "And now we begin our tour of the famous Bluff City."

Mignonne chattered incessantly, pointing out beautiful churches and telling Adrianna about the people who lived in the various mansions.

Subdued, Adrianna commented on the beautiful Greek Revival houses, but she was accustomed to seeing such houses in her native Georgia. As they walked their horses beneath dripping trees along Randolph Street, she watched this pair so eagerly trying to entertain her. Of course, Adrianna was the granddaughter of someone important to Foy's business. He had amused himself yesterday by playing Sir Galahad.

With a sigh, she pulled her eyes from his strong, sharp profile and glanced up, up three stories to a cupola surrounded by a captain's walk. "This one's different," she said, struggling to be pleasant. "One doesn't expect to see Italianate architecture in the middle of the countryside."

"Actually, we're quite near the river," said Mignonne. "The Simpsons could watch for their steamboats from up there. My mother —"

"I'm so glad you like this style," Foy interrupted, beaming at her.

"Yes." She felt warmed by his smile.

"Italianate architecture was in vogue during the 1850s when Eufaula was a flourishing shipping point." He spoke eagerly, openly relieved that she was interested again. "Cotton went to Europe, and returning boats brought French and English furniture and Italian marble. If we can just get a few problems resolved, it will be that way again!"

"You'll manage," she replied. "I've never known anyone as sure of what he wanted to do."

A slow smile spread over his serious face. "Come on. I want to show you Barbour Hall." He kneed his horse to a brisk canter.

Feeling safe with the sureness of his leading, Adrianna followed, the ribbons of her hat streaming as they rode along the river bluff. Exhilarated by the speed, she was sorry when they turned the corner at Barbour Street and slowed again.

"That's the Keils's house," Mignonne said in a stage whisper. "It has hand paintings on the walls and silver doorknobs!"

"And gold window cornices which match the pier mirrors," said Foy. "You can build in a grand manner when you're stealing tax revenue." He spat out his words bitterly.

Adrianna glanced up to the cupola.

Following her gaze, Foy said, "It's rumored there are holes in the cupola for rifles to shoot through. And see that door under the front steps? I've heard there's a secret passage on the first floor, and—uh-oh."

A woman's figure stirred in the high bay window.

"Let's move on. Everyone knows I was at Spring Hill. Mrs. Keils can't help her husband's bribes and crooked schemes. I sadly regret that the little boy is wounded."

As they approached Barbour Hall, small, cold drops of rain stung their cheeks. Foy spoke in a melancholy tone. "For ten years we've lived with lawlessness that has made gun-toting a necessity. My life has been standing still!"

The earnestness on his face melted the reserve Adrianna had thrown around her heart at the threat of Mignonne. Now she knew why so desirable a man had remained unmarried. Entering his home, she resolved that if he wanted nothing more, she would give him friendship.

"Oh, how beautiful!" she exclaimed in genuine appreciation as she stepped into the elegant spaciousness of the central hall. "It must be wonderful to have a place preserved through generations. I've never had a permanent home." For a moment she thought of all the places and people with whom she had stayed. She had never felt stable or secure. She shook off her wistfulness and smiled. "This marble floor is so dramatic!" She gestured across the black and white diamonds which stretched the entire length of the house.

"I like the crown of thorns chandelier," said Mignonne softly. She pointed up to the ring of six-pointed stars stabbed with crystal thorns and hung with teardrops.

Casually Adrianna glanced at it, thinking that these people were a bit provincial in the way they brought religion into their everyday life.

She followed Foy to the right into the music room. "How lovely!" She clasped her fingertips together in delight. Crossing to the square, rosewood piano, she rippled a tune on the keys. "Who's the musician in the family?"

"Emma's the most accomplished." Foy smiled down at her, obviously pleased that she liked his home.

"Emma?" She paused, struggling to remember. "Ramsey? Your family?"

Foy laughed. "Of course. She's my aunt. She was Lily's chaperone. My nursemaid. Everyone loves Emma."

"Well, I declare," she murmured. As she absorbed the reason Emma had looked at Foy so lovingly, happiness swelled within her. With a flood of tenderness, she smiled at the thick hair curling around his ears.

Pointing at the crystal chandelier over the long mahogany table in the dining room, Foy stopped talking midsentence as if he could feel her eyes upon him. He turned, mistook her hands clasped to her heart, and said, "But you must be cold. Come to the fire."

Mignonne disappeared into the back hall as Foy ushered Adrianna across to the parlor.

Sitting gracefully on a small settee close to the white marble fireplace, Adrianna smiled at Foy as he dropped to one knee on the hearth. Dry oak logs lay smoldering, giving no warmth.

From a brass basket, Foy took a splinter of fat, lightwood kindling. "This fat li'dard will get a roaring fire going." He touched a match to the pine splinter. It flared. Quickly poking the blazing sliver between the logs, he sat back on his heels with satisfaction as rich pine tar sizzled fiery trails over the dry logs.

"I should have realized you'd be cold and wet." Foy looked up at her, his lean face full of concern.

"I'm fine," Adrianna assured him. Spreading her hands toward the flickering blaze, she leaned toward Foy. Leaping blue and yellow flames filled the fireplace, roared in her ears. Aromatic steam rose from the wet wool at Foy's shoulder. "I'm just . . . fine." Her voice dropped to a whisper.

"I'm sorry I didn't realize sooner that . . ." His breath caught as his dark eyes searched hers.

Tremulously, she met the force of his gaze. For a suspended moment they remained dangerously close to the popping, crackling fire.

Shaken by the feelings setting her face aglow, Adrianna

drew back from the blaze. She swallowed, tried to speak. "Really, I . . ."

Foy's face was close beside hers as he remained kneeling before her. He breathed deeply of her perfume. "I've questioned . . ." He gazed at her wonderingly and his hand lifted, trembled inches from her cheek. "Why my life has been suspended. Perhaps," his voice broke huskily. "Perhaps, without knowing it, I've been waiting for you."

Motionless, Adrianna stared at him. Surely she had misunderstood his whispered words. But, no, she could not mistake the feeling of his eyes caressing her face.

A rattle, a thump sounded from the hallway. Neither moved, but Adrianna slowly lifted her eyes to the image in the gold leaf mirror behind Foy. Pushing the mahogany tea cart as if she owned it, Mignonne was speculatively eyeing them.

Sighing, Adrianna took the cup of tea which Mignonne poured with practiced skill. Bowing her head over the steaming brew, she took comfort from it as the scent of cinnamon and apples bathed her face. She must control her turbulent emotions. She had only known this man for twenty-four hours, yet she was falling in love with him.

"I have a surprise!" Foy's eyes twinkled as he set his cup the mantel. "Something both you girls will love. Adrianna's grandfather has agreed to take a trip up the Chattahoochee! We're all going to see—"

"Ohhhh," cried Adrianna. "It sounds so exciting, but," she sighed and gestured as she talked. "Ma-ma will never go."

Adrianna's eyes danced. It was not friendship she wanted from this man. It was love. The uncharted course before her might be as filled with rocks and hidden shoals as the treacherous Chattahoochee, but she was eager to face the dangers.

four

Your grandmother will surely want to go," Foy said, "when I tell her that 'Le Sphinx' starring Alice D. Lengard will be opening at the Springer Saturday night."

Adrianna hesitated. "The Springer?"

"The Springer Opera House," he said quickly. "It was only built three years ago. Already it's known as the finest between New York and New Orleans. Harrison has reserved a box."

Mignonne clapped delightedly.

"However did you know that theater is the one thing Mama could not resist?" Laughter bubbled in Adrianna's voice.

"I guessed." Foy smiled at her pleasure.

Companionably, they helped themselves to pastries and settled around the crackling fire to plan their trip. At last Lige was summoned to bring around the carriage. They rode to the hotel through a downpour of cold, gray rain, but Adrianna's heart was filled with sunshine.

Rain continued the next morning. Cross from the pain the weather gave her, Isadora Atherton kept Adrianna jumping to satisfy her whims. By afternoon, Isadora had become peevish that no one was according her attention. When at four o'clock a knock sounded at the door to their suite, Adrianna was delighted to admit Lily Wingate.

After the customary small talk, Lily inclined her dark head and said sadly, "I've come from visiting Mrs. Keils."

"You did?" Adrianna asked in surprise.

"Sometimes you have to turn the other cheek," Lily said self-consciously. "I felt so sorry for her. Little Willie died just now. Our son, Harrison Junior, is nine. When I think how she must feel . . ." Her voice choked with sympathy. "Isn't it sad how often wrongdoing makes the innocent suffer?"

"What will happen to the scalawag?" asked Adrianna. "Or have they already strung him up?"

"Adrianna!" exclaimed Isadora, shocked.

"That's all right." Lily's tone assured her that she was not offended by youthful directness. "He's been taken to Montgomery where they'll begin impeachment proceedings."

Isadora patted her perfectly arranged hair disinterestedly and murmured, "I'm sure there will be a congressional investigation. The Senator will—" She broke off.

"Yes. Well," Lily nodded. "A fine, honest man, General Alpheus Baker, one of our war heroes, was running against him. Harrison says that when he is declared judge . . . Maybe now our lives can begin again."

Foy's voice seemed to whisper in Adrianna's ear. "I've wondered why my life has been suspended. Perhaps, without knowing it, I've been waiting for you."

Slowly she traced his initials on her cheek with the tip of her finger as she listened to his sister explaining the plans for the trip to Columbus, Georgia, at the head of the Chattahoochee.

"There has been plenty of rain upstream," Lily said in her bright, vivacious way. "The river is high and reasonably safe. You need not worry." She laughed lightly. "The year Harrison and I married there was a drought. The river dropped so low that he had a terrible time getting here for our wedding."

Adrianna noticed how often and how lovingly Lily spoke her husband's name. She marveled again at the closeness of their marriage. It was hard to believe this young-looking woman had been married sixteen years and had a nine-year-old son.

Friday morning dawned crisp and clear. Thumbing through her extensive wardrobe, Adrianna decided to don the same bottle-green costume she had worn on Tuesday. She hoped it would remind Foy of their first meeting.

Excitedly she helped her grandmother board the omnibus which would take them to the steamboat landing. As they swung around the curving road which descended the steep bluff, the clang of the bell and the high-pitched wheet-wheet of the whistle made her lean forward.

"They won't leave us, Adrianna," Senator Atherton laughed.

Suddenly they reached the clearing, and she could see the tremendous, flat-bottomed boat with its lower deck just above the water's edge. Other decks mounted up like stair steps. Above all towered the smokestacks. Swinging between them, a sign proclaimed the name *New Jackson*. Passengers surged across the clearing, scrambled down the bank, and sprawled over the lower deck heedless of the stevedores who strained bulging muscles to load the last of the freight. Separating from the group, Mignonne leaned far out over the rail and waved her handkerchief.

Uhmmm! Uhm! Uhmmmm! The deep, rumbling blast of the steamboat's whistle made Adrianna jump.

She felt his presence and turned. Foy smiled and said something that was swallowed by the whistle echoing and reechoing around them. They laughed. They had no need for words. Foy's eyes lighted as he drank in her appearance. His slight nod as his glance flicked over the vibrant green dress told her he remembered. Glad she had no need to speak, she mentally re-created the sensation of their flight on horseback when she had been held tightly against him.

The crowd parted as her handsome grandparents moved grandly toward the gangplank. The distinguished-looking Senator towered six inches above most of the men whom he greeted with quick handshakes. Isadora Atherton's voluptuous figure, laced into an extremely full bustle, showed to perfection. Her high-billed bonnet completed the odd, goose-shaped fashion of the day.

Forgotten by her kin as usual, Adrianna lagged behind. Foy stepped closer in the crush of chattering people, grasped her elbow, and helped her over the gangway and up the stairs to the first class deck.

The huge water wheel at the stern of the boat strained, reversed, and backed the craft into the channel. Settling into a rhythmic swish, swish, swish, the wheel threw rainbow mists into the air and left a foaming white wake behind.

Dizzied by the movement and exhilaration, Adrianna grasped the wooden rail. Foy's hand brushed hers, as if accidentally, then settled two inches down the rail, far enough for decorum, close enough to make the hairs on the back of her hand tingle.

"Direct your eyes straight ahead." He spoke softly as the boat glided in peaceful silence.

"Oh, it's glorious!" Enchanted, Adrianna stretched both hands toward the huge golden leaves of the sycamores which knelt at the water's edge. Behind them, deep red sweet gums clung to the slope. Stalwart brown oaks lined the crest of the bluff that was Alabama. "There's a mysterious feeling," she exclaimed. "Like floating through fairyland."

Smiling at her with satisfaction, Foy replied, "Nothing quite matches the feeling of a paddlewheeler on a beautiful river. Look," he said, pointing. "Speaking of matching . . ."

She turned toward Georgia. The huge red ball of sun rising behind bottle-green pines set fire to translucent maple leaves. Tenderly he reached one finger to brush a red-gold strand tumbling over her forehead. "Maple leaves in autumn," he whispered. "Springtime in my heart."

Adrianna glowed from the sunlight of happiness rising within her.

Weaving toward them from the bow of the boat, Mignonne came all achatter. Foy dropped his hand to the wooden rail. "Our steamer will have brass rails," he said enthusiastically. "White fretwork trim. Even a mahogany dance floor!"

"And guess what?" Mignonne interposed. "She's named for me!"

Adrianna felt as if the deck had collapsed. Voices sounded muted, hollow.

"I can't wait to get to the iron works and show her to you!" Foy exclaimed.

"I'll bet Foy'll never call her Minnie." Mignonne stuck the tip of her pink tongue out at him. The conversation continued, but Adrianna had withdrawn into her own misery. Evidently she had mistaken Foy's natural warmth and little-boy sweetness for romantic interest. If his boat were named for Mignonne, they must be engaged. Suddenly she realized that they were watching her expectantly.

"I . . . uh," she stammered. "I guess I'd better . . . Ma-ma will be wanting me. Please excuse . . ." Head high, Adrianna walked quickly toward her grandmother. Even though the boat glided smoothly, she felt dizzy. Numbly she planned her only course. She would compliment their boat. She would attend the theater party. Then she would catch a train at Columbus and go home.

Mother wants me. That's what I'll say. She clamped her teeth resolutely. She could not bear a return trip near Foy in the romantic aura of the river if he were pledged to another.

She joined Isadora who was reclining on a wicker chaise longue in the ladies' saloon.

"Mother has written for me to come home." The lie rolled from Adrianna's tongue, hot, bitter.

"*I* need you," Isadora snapped, obviously annoyed at the inconvenience it would cause her.

Trying to keep their tense voices from carrying to the other ladies, they argued. At last Isadora consented to Adrianna's plan to leave from Columbus.

With both hands to her aching head, the girl realized miserably that her mother might not want to be bothered with her.

Just as she rose murmuring that she wanted to lie down, Adrianna was thrown back. The steamer lurched. Wood splintered; women wailed.

"We're sinking," Isadora shrieked and fell back in a swoon.

Adrianna ran to a window and saw burly Captain Fry rushing below, his arms piled high with pillows and blankets.

"Mark my words," a sharp-faced woman beside

Adrianna said with a sniff. "You will never feel safe with a Fry as captain!"

Startled, Adrianna raised quizzical eyebrows.

Thus encouraged, the woman continued in a gossipy voice, "Yes, my dear, didn't you know the Fry brothers were accused of being Yankee sympathizers?"

The boat dropped slightly and settled with a shudder. Adrianna rushed back to waft smelling salts beneath Isadora's nose. Should she take her grandmother to her cabin and loosen her corset? Frantically, Adrianna looked toward a large, motherly woman who smiled reassuringly.

"I think, ladies, that we should move outside to the rails in case quitting the boat becomes necessary," she said.

The sharp-nosed woman looked at the prostrate Isadora and sniffed disdainfully. "Don't upset yourself. The river here is shallow enough to wade. As I was saying, the Frys had their licenses suspended during the war. I always wondered—"

"Now, Gussie," interrupted another woman. "The Frys proved themselves innocent."

Adrianna was amazed that the seasoned travelers seemed interested only in gossiping. Conversation stopped when Dan Fry reappeared. "No cause for alarm, folks," he shouted. "She struck a snag, but we staunched the hole. Praise be, we're now grounded on a sandbar, and we'll have her fixed in jig time."

Astounded that the captain had saved his boat with mere feathers, wool, and sand, Adrianna noted the inadequacy of her own knowledge. Perhaps she could hold Foy's interest better if she knew more things outside herself.

Long after the hole was repaired, the *New Jackson* remained stranded in the shallow spot in the river. Plans were made to transfer the passengers to the *GWE Wiley*. Suddenly the river rose slightly from a freshet upstream and the flat boat lifted from the sandbar.

That afternoon with the boat underway, Lily joined Adrianna and Isadora on the shady side of the deck. Her rosy-cheeked son, whom everyone called Beau, asked permission to go to the pilothouse. Watching his bobbing, sun-streaked hair as he scampered up the stairs, Adrianna thought tenderly that his Uncle Foy must have looked like him.

Breaking her mood, Mignonne plopped into the chair beside her.

"I'm so glad Papa let me stay out of school," Mignonne said. "It's the first time I've ever met anyone sophisticated like you."

Adrianna laughed. The girl would be surprised to know just how unsure of herself she felt. "School?" she murmured. "I thought you'd finished." Her eyes came into focus on the beautiful girl, and she asked, "How old are you?"

"Fourteen."

"I'd guessed sixteen, you're so lovely—seventeen, even."

"She is blossoming early," said Lily.

For a moment Adrianna's hopes rose. Clearly Mignonne was too young for Foy. But he could have fallen in love with her and be waiting for her to make her debut, to present herself at the marriageable age of sixteen. Obviously there was warmth between them. She rubbed her glare-dazzled eyes and tried to turn her attention to where Lily was pointing.

"Look, look!" Lily gestured as the steamboat nudged

through a tunnel of trees and slid beside a clearing. " 'Look on the fields; for they are white already to harvest,' " she quoted. Then she added softly, "But the laborers are few."

Puzzled, Adrianna moved to the rail to see. She stared across a field of cotton. It was snow white, certainly, yet many workers moved through the rows.

"Don't mind Lily." Foy's deep voice vibrated behind her ear. "She knows a Scripture for every occasion."

Adrianna could see fondness and pride in the look Foy gave his sister. She coughed to cover her embarrassment that she had not known Lily was quoting the Bible. This family's faith seemed such a deep and abiding part of their lives that she feared their derision because of the little religious training she had received.

Foy joined her at the rail, and together they leaned toward the entrancing view. Pickers passing down rows on one side of the field began a chanting song. An answering melody came from deep, rolling voices in another group, and the chant rippled back and forth across the field. The music drifted over the water and encircled the young couple.

Smiling up at Foy's face, Adrianna said, "I wish I could paint that scene."

"You're an artist?"

"Oh, no. But I'd like to be. Perhaps I should study. I just haven't decided."

Foy smiled down at her and said lightly, "It's important to have a goal." He laughed and gestured. "Of course, I probably have too many. But when I see a field of cotton like that I have hope. Some of the planters are getting land that was overgrown during the war back in shape for a bumper crop. If I can buy and store their cotton and then ship it myself as well—"

"I thought the *Mig*, er, your steamer, was for luxury travel."

"That's just the cream." Foy laughed. "It's shipping freight that pays the bills. You see if we can get into both sides of the business. . . " Foy's eyes burned as he shared his plans and dreams.

That evening at dinner, the senior members of their party sat at Captain Dan Fry's table. Adrianna, Mignonne, and Foy joined a younger group. Adrianna bit into crisply battered fried chicken. Roasted venison was passed next. Oysters were served in abundance. She lost track of what she ate as, through the many courses, Foy joked and teased.

After dinner, the laughing group moved into the grand saloon for dancing. With Foy's arms whirling her giddily in a waltz and music filling her senses, Adrianna forgot Mignonne, forgot everything but the thrill of Foy's touch and his strong hand holding hers.

At last, breathlessly, they went onto the deck to cool. Stars twinkled magically around them. The boat tugged slightly at her mooring.

"Your eyes are like the Chattahoochee," Foy said softly. "Ever changing. At supper they were as blue and soft as your gown. Now they're dark as the night river." He leaned closer.

His breath was warm and sweet against her face for moments measured by moonbeams. The melody of the rushing river as it paused to play among the rocks intensified her longing for his love. Her innocent lips trembled as she lifted her face toward his and hoped for his kiss.

Voices drifted around them. Foy straightened, moved away.

"But this morning," he laughed shakily as time began again to tick. "This morning your eyes were like the river at its clearest—green!"

"Green as envy," she laughed ruefully, "when I heard you'd named your boat for Mignonne. Don't you think," she frowned, suddenly angered that the enchanted moment had been shattered by people spilling around them.

"That's silly!" Astounded, Foy stared at her. "I couldn't know I'd meet you and fall—"

"That fourteen is too young for—" The tart sound of her voice surprised her, but it continued. "You must be all of twenty-five."

"I'm twenty-eight," he said between stiff lips. "And you?"

"Eighteen, nearly nineteen!"

Surprise showed on his face. "I thought you nearer my age. You're so sophisticated."

A harsh laugh rattled in her throat as he used Mignonne's term. "Oh, I've traveled a lot." *From one parent to another*, she thought bitterly. Fighting tears, she seemed unable to keep her manner from chilling into haughtiness. Like a falling star, their shimmering closeness plummeted, extinguished.

"Foy. Foyee, come on." Mignonne was tugging at his hand. "Miss Adrianna, they're wanting everyone to line up for a cotillion."

The next day Foy joined Adrianna on deck. "We're nearly to Race Pass," he said with a serious expression which seemed to shut her out. "I'll show you the grave of the *Chattahoochee*."

"The river's grave?" Puzzled by his words and his

distant attitude, she lifted her eyebrows.

"Our gunboat," he said in a voice of deep melancholy.
"We had to sink her to keep the Yankees from taking her."

Suddenly the huge paddle wheels shuddered to a stop.
Adrianna leaned over the rail to peer through the muddy
water. She could see only a tip of the sunken hull, and she
watched breathlessly as the *New Jackson* grazed slowly by
it with a horrifying scraping sound.

"Whew!" Adrianna whistled. "I hadn't understood what
you meant about the dangers of obstructions. I do now!"

"She's waiting to drag another steamer down with her all
right," Foy replied dourly.

"How did you get away after you sank her?"

"Escaping the Yankees was no problem. We were a crew
with no ship." He rubbed his furrowed eyebrows. "Some
of us went west to try and join General Nathan Bedford
Forrest. We didn't know the war was over. I was gone when
Emma needed me most. I always seem to have bad timing." He regarded her with an unreadable look and repeated, "Bad timing."

That evening in the finest hotel suite in Columbus,
Georgia, Adrianna dressed with care. Wanting to restore
the light in Foy's eyes, she chose a lavishly draped gown
of lustrous pink satin. As she brushed perfume on her warm
skin, she was glad that the pink from too much sun had
faded to a golden glow. Pulling on elbow length, white kid
gloves, she appraised herself from every angle. A small
tiara was fastened into the crown of sparkling curls piled
high upon her head. She looked taller, older. Her reflection
in the looking glass pleased her until she leaned closer and
noticed six new freckles marching across her nose.

When she entered the hotel lobby, Foy's face lifted in delight.

"Good evening, fairy princess." Foy inhaled appreciatively and bowed to kiss her fingertips. As he slowly lifted his head, his dark eyes touched lingeringly on each new freckle with the feel of a kiss. He chuckled softly.

"Good evening," drawled a honeyed voice.

Reluctantly, they turned. Mignonne bobbed a curtsy to Adrianna's elegance. Her long curls bounced like coffee-colored springs.

" 'Lo, Miggie," Foy said. He reached out and tugged a curl.

"Not Miggie," the girl wailed in mock horror. "Minnie's bad enough!" She wrinkled her pert nose at him.

Adrianna withdrew from them into her soul. As she moved mechanically to the waiting carriage, she felt achingly alone. Whenever they snatched a private moment, she felt certain that Foy was as overwhelmed with passion as she. But an intangible snag seemed to jut between them each time they drew near. If he were pledged to Mignonne, the only honorable thing for her to do was leave. *Tomorrow*, she thought resolutely to herself as she stepped from the carriage in front of the Springer Opera House.

Emerging in their private box, she looked about the theater and exclaimed, "Why, it's just like Ford's Theater in Washington!"

"I'm so glad you approve," Foy said. Holding a velvet chair at the brass rail for her, he then seated himself close behind.

Adrianna tried to concentrate on Mrs. Lengard's fine acting, but each time Foy leaned forward to comment, his breath was warm against her bare shoulder.

As the first act's crisis gripped everyone's attention, Adrianna had the uneasy sensation someone was watching her. Looking down into the darkened theater, she could distinguish no one, however outlined against the gold box by the lights from the stage, her bright hair and pink dress were clearly visible.

When the house lights came up at the end of the act, she saw him just as his gaze turned toward Lily. His features had the chiseled perfection of a Greek statue.

Adrianna noticed Lily blushing, her poise obviously shaken. Adrianna's own skin reddened when the man's attention returned to her. His eyes roamed lazily over her, causing her to feel that he could see the flowers embroidered on her corset cover. Flapping her ivory fan angrily, she snapped her head around.

Harrison Wingate, always unperturbable, acknowledged the man with a quick salute, but when his hand dropped to his side, his fist clenched.

Mignonne's response was innocence, Isadora's experience, Senator Atherton's a jovial façade. Foy Edwards puzzled her most. The reddened tips of his ears and the knitting of his heavy brows betrayed anger.

Adrianna heard none of the second act. Although she kept her face coolly turned toward the stage, she could feel the man's eyes often upon her. She kept wondering who this irritating, fascinating man could be who had everyone in their box sitting on a razor's edge of emotion.

When the house lights came on for intermission, he had disappeared.

five

Gaslights illumined the theater. A babble of voices floated up to their silent box. The private door opened. He entered.

Tension crackled. After a long moment, Harrison leaned around his wife, offering his hand. Ignored, his big hand seemed to hang suspended.

The man's golden curls bobbed in a curt nod. He laughed. "Harrison, old man, still trying to be the stalwart steamboat captain, I heah." His cultured voice had the unmistakable accent of Charleston. He laughed again and swiftly thrust out his hand to shake Harrison's now limp fingers.

Quickly he turned his gaze upon Lily. "Why Lily, honey," he said, grasping both her shoulders and holding her back in genuine admiration. "What a beautiful woman you've become!" He kissed her warmly on the cheek.

Obviously flustered, Lily stammered, "Why, Green, how—what a surprise! I . . . we'd heard you were no longer in cotton—"

"No, cotton factoring is not the most lucrative . . ."

"Humph!" Foy snorted close behind Adrianna's ear. "The way he practiced it, filthy lucre is more the word!"

Over her concealing fan, Adrianna noted the man's elegantly tailored clothes. Although he was a few years older than Foy, he remained trim. Only a slight puffiness around his eyes and a glazed look indicated dissipation.

He finished answering Lily and turned toward Adrianna.

"I'm forgetting my manners," Lily said quickly. "Senator and Mrs. Atherton, may I present my distant cousin, Green Bethune." Her voice flattened. "From South Carolina."

"Senator Atherton, I'm honored to make your acquaintance, sir." He shook hands quickly, then interrupted the Senator's reply to bow over Isadora's fingertips. "And yours, beautiful lady. And this must be your daughter."

Isadora's delicate face could not hide her gratification at the compliment to her agelessness. "Adrianna, dear," she slipped her arm around Adrianna's waist and imperceptibly shoved her forward. "Mr. Bethune."

"Miss Adrianna!" He kissed her hand correctly. "What a lovely name!" He smiled familiarly as he squeezed her fingers in private greeting.

A thrill of excitement quivered over her at his obvious interest and the tangible jealousy from Foy who stood fuming behind her. Adrianna flashed her most dazzling smile and cooed, "How do you do, Mr. Bethune. Don't I detect the voice of Charleston?" She withdrew her hand.

"Do you know our city?" he replied eagerly. "She's suffered greatly, but she's still the center of our beau monde!"

"Oh, I quite agree, sir," Adrianna said coyly. Batting her eyelashes in an inviting glance, she thought that if this charming older man paid her court, Foy should reconsider his concerns about their age difference. Searching for something to hold Green's attention, she let honey drip from her words. "I do adore Charleston's fine old houses and gardens. It's just marvelous they weren't destroyed in that awful war—"

"Green." Lily interrupted. "You do remember Foy? And

this—"

"Well, well, he's grown a yard since I've seen him." Green Bethune laughed mirthlessly as he nodded to Foy. His eyes slid past him to the beautiful girl.

"And this," Lily repeated, "is our daughter, Mignonne. Young Harrison is at the hotel—in bed, I hope."

Mignonne extended her hand prettily, but her lip protruded petulantly at Green's words.

"What a pretty *child*," he said. "So like your mother when I knew her."

Gaslights dimming signaled the last act was about to begin. Bethune turned quickly to include the whole group. "You all must be my guests for a late supper after the play. No, I insist." He waved down their protests. "I won't take no for an answer." As he left their box, Green Bethune's eyes once again swept over Adrianna, devouring her.

Thankful for the darkness, Adrianna sank miserably into her chair. She had led him on. Deliberately! It was as if she had imitated Isadora. Hot color drained from her cheeks as she realized what she had let jealousy do to her. From the corner of her eye, she could see Foy's fist clenching and unclenching. Mignonne's proprietary air over Foy had made her feel threatened. She had seen Mignonne as another woman. Peeping around her fan at Mignonne, she now saw a pouting child, a child with a crush on an adored uncle.

Squirming, she thought the show would never end, yet she feared its conclusion. She had begun a flirtation with this worldly man that she lacked experience to handle.

Adrianna's long fingernails bit into her palms. She felt certain that Foy had been falling in love with her. What must he think of her now?

In the fashionable restaurant, Adrianna sipped coffee and toyed with rich, chocolate pie. Green Bethune had managed to seat her beside himself. She gazed beseechingly at Foy, but he sat with Mignonne at the far end of the table.

Most of the conversation flowed between Green Bethune and Senator Atherton, both of whom were accustomed to dominating any gathering. Saying nothing, behaving as inconspicuously as possible, Adrianna was careful to turn no inviting glances upon Green. She barely listened until he raised his voice to claim everyone's attention and explain his reason for being in Columbus.

"Of course, I still have my shipping line to Liverpool," Green said. "But until cotton regains its kingship, I'm dabbling in insurance, helping out a firm from New York City."

"How did that come about?" asked Harrison, trying to ease a noticeably tense situation.

Green laughed. "Since the War of Northern Aggression, some northern insurance companies have given positions to southern war heroes." He paused to let his audience absorb his intimation. "To create good will in the South. It's taken a great deal of work to pay off claims on Confederate dead and reinstate lapsed policies."

Adrianna noticed Foy muttering something to no one in particular. She tried to catch his eye, but he would not look at her. Sitting stiffly with a false smile fixed upon her face, she jumped as she heard her name mentioned.

"Mrs. Atherton, may I have your permission to call upon Miss Adrianna tomorrow?"

Isadora responded to Green's charm. "I would be delighted for such a fine gentleman to call." She tilted her head coyly. "But this independent *child* is leaving us tomorrow."

Stricken, Adrianna sat staring at her plate. She scarcely knew how she endured the rest of the evening.

As they left the restaurant, Foy brushed against her. "You're leaving? I thought you promised to see my steamboat!"

"I did. I'm going to," she answered in a small voice. "Foy, I must explain."

Suddenly everyone was moving purposefully, saying good night, sweeping them apart.

Feeling that winter had descended, Adrianna dressed warmly in aquamarine velvet with white fur trim. Weak and sick from crying, she peered in the mirror at her red, swollen eyes and blotched face. She would never see Foy after this morning, and this was how he would remember her. If he remembered her.

"Oh, Foy, I love you so much!" she whispered.

Images of his face when first they met moved slowly as she savored the bittersweetness. He had felt the same impact. He had fallen in love with her, but in anger and jealousy she had retreated into icy silence.

How often had her father taken her by the shoulders and said, "Adrianna, you're becoming moody again. You're holding things inside and your attitude is growing worse each day. Let it out."

They would talk out her problems. She would cry, feel better, be her sunny self again. If only she could talk with him now. The rest of the family loved her in their own ways, but her father listened. Since her parents had separated, she did not even know where he was.

The rattling of a table being rolled into the sitting room told her breakfast had arrived. Time was running out.

The sitting room was filled with Senator Atherton's voice as he conferred with aides. Isadora lounged in a French negligee, seemingly unperturbed that everyone else was dressed to go out.

"You're not going?" asked Adrianna, suddenly fearful that she would miss seeing Foy this last time.

"It's just another steamboat." Isadora shrugged.

"But I promised to . . ." Her voice broke.

"Oh, you can go with your grandfather," Isadora said brusquely, noticing Adrianna's crestfallen face, "but I'm entirely too fatigued to wear myself out further when I won't be having you to—Oh, my poor, poor fingers," she wailed and displayed a trembling hand.

"Oh, Ma-ma, let me stay with you! Oh, not this morning. I mean stay. You need me—I'll telegraph Mother that I'm not coming, and . . ."

Isadora eyed her thoughtfully. "I'd like to have you." She wavered. "But, no. She's expecting you. Arrangements have been made. Your traveling companion, Mrs. Cristie, will be here at noon. I'm sorry, Adrianna, but you're always changing your mind and now it's too late!"

The steamboat floated like a white palace. Emblazoned between towering black smokestacks was the name *Mignonne Wingate* and the emblem of a descending dove. Adrianna bit her lip.

Hand high over his head, Foy waved. He bounded over the gangway to her side. "You came!" he cried. "Tell me you're not leaving."

"I—" She searched his face. If only he would speak

the words she longed to hear. "I asked Ma-ma to let me stay." She swallowed. "But she said arrangements . . . I want to stay with—I want to ride the *Mignonne*—Oh, Foy, I've acted so silly! I thought you were engaged to her, and—"

"What?" He twisted his face incredulously. "Good grannies, woman!" As the Senator's group came on board, Foy gestured wildly, sorely torn. Jerking a nod toward Harrison, who escorted the men down the deck, Foy grasped Adrianna's elbow and muttered, "Let's go somewhere we can talk. I'll show you the pilothouse."

Silently they climbed the tiers of decks to the glass tower. Alone at last, they stood a pace apart not knowing what to say.

Foy broke the painful silence. "How could you think I was engaged to a child I've loved and cared for since birth?"

"I could see you loved each other, but—"

"You know Lily is my sister."

"She's so young looking. Mignonne is so beautiful. Remember, I met you all during the riot, and with her hanging on your arm all the time and, and the boat named for her, how could I know she was your niece? I assumed you were betrothed. That's why I had to lie about—"

"Lie?" Foy's brows, which had begun to relax with understanding, knitted again.

With tear-filled eyes, Adrianna searched his serious face. If only he would gather her in his arms and let her cry out her heartache as Papa had done. Miserably she looked down at her clasping hands and mumbled, "I had to get away. Loving you . . ." She swallowed. "Seeing you pledged to another—I had to make up that my mother had sent for me."

The wind whistled through the door of the pilothouse. Adrianna shivered, leaning hopefully toward Foy. He said nothing. Slowly she raised her head. His hands hung limply at his sides. Unreadable emotions played over his face. She longed to trace his cheekbone with her fingertips, to kiss the reddened rims of his ears. In his smoldering eyes, she saw pain.

His voice broke huskily when at last he spoke. "We need time—time together. I've got such plans. Can't you . . ." Hesitatingly his hands came up, grasped her shoulders. He looked down into her face and said urgently, "Can't you explain? Stay here!"

"The arrangements are made. My grandfather is a benevolent Santa Claus at times. At others, he's as hard and unyielding as—God. He'd make me go to punish the lie."

Foy frowned. "I don't agree with your concept of God. But, Adrianna, any lie is always wrong, always causes hurting, and—"

She wrenched from his grip. "What is truth?" She twisted her mouth scornfully.

"Truth is—Adrianna, don't get off on a tangent. I can't quote you chapter and verse like Lily does, but I know Jesus said, 'I am the way, the truth.' There are so many things we need to talk about." Foy's strong tanned hands cupped her trembling cheeks as he whispered, "Oh, my beautiful Adrianna, please—"

"Good morning, you two," a cheery voice sang out from the deck below.

"Green!" Foy spat out the words as he dropped his hands.

"Who *is* that man?" Adrianna stamped her foot.

"Mama had arranged for Lily to marry him, but Lily had the good sense to choose Harrison. Green shot Harrison in a duel!"

Shocked, Adrianna recoiled. Foy's sharp features were frozen in fury. His heavy brows were drawn down, shutting her out. She began to shake as she realized she had told Foy she loved him, yet he had made no such declaration. With a flip of her veil, she turned her back.

As the door opened and Green Bethune entered the pilothouse, Adrianna smiled, smiled far too much. Because Foy seemed to hate this man, she put a false warmth into her voice. "Good morning, Mr. Bethune!"

He doffed his round, hard hat and bowed over her hand, kissing it lingeringly. "How delightful to see you. I rose early this morning hoping to catch you before you left. Your hat and gown remind me of the waters and warmth of the Gulf. Have you taken the cruise down to the bay?"

"I—no, I haven't seen it." She withdrew her hand and tucked it into her white fur muff. "I'd hoped to take an excursion while. . ." She peered over Green's shoulder, beseeching Foy.

The tautness of his skin over the sharp bones of his face bespoke hurt pride, cold anger. Suddenly he whirled, stalked to the door, and stamped down the steep stairway.

She would not want Foy shot in a duel, but she was disappointed that he was not staying to fight his adversary. Speaking loud enough to carry, she flung out, "I think perhaps I'd rather go to New York."

"Winter in the city is a cultural enrichment," Green nodded. "Perhaps I could escort you to the theater."

Foy dropped from sight.

Edging uneasily away from Green Bethune, Adrianna

stared down at a lone dogwood tree on the river bank. Green followed her to the window, but suddenly his intimate manner changed. "I admire your independent spirit," he said seriously. "You call to mind Susan B. Anthony, and I thought—"

Flattered, Adrianna turned. Perhaps this man understood her. "She is my idol. How did you guess?"

Smoothly, he preened his side whiskers. "I suspected as much. As a champion of women's rights, she works against laws which keep women from achieving financial independence. A friend of mine sold her a life insurance policy back in 1855."

Adrianna looked at him in surprise. "I didn't know women bought life insurance."

"Few realize the power of this avenue to money, the available collateral. I felt that if apprised of the opportunity, you would want to buy a policy."

Adrianna's mouth dropped open as he quickly took papers from a case. *What a vain and foolish creature I've been in thinking his interest personal!* She laughed harshly. "I'm sorry to disappoint you, Mr. Bethune, but I have no funds whatsoever."

"You jest." He touched a finger to her fur collar. "Let me explain how—"

"Mr. Bethune, I have no money at all. My grandfather lavishes presents to bring credit upon himself. If I want something, I have to justify—"

"That is exactly the reason women need—"

"Mr. Bethune," she said icily. "I don't have a penny to call my own." She stepped from the tower with as much dignity as she could muster.

Cold wind whipped her veil. Clutching her hat as she

descended to the hurricane deck, Adrianna headed toward the sound of her grandfather's voice. Trailing after his party which Foy was now leading, she said nothing. When she occasionally looked out from the icy recesses of her soul, the proud indifference she saw on Foy's averted profile chilled her marrow.

Like a sleepwalker, Adrianna moved through the rest of the morning until she found herself at the train depot. Suddenly a hiss of steam swirled around Adrianna's skirt. She had stumbled too close to the iron locomotive. A flying cinder seared her eye. Crying out, stopping to dig at it, she was tugged through the train depot by Mrs. Cristie.

"Wait. Wait. Please wait," she begged. Looking back over her shoulder, she ached to see Foy, to hear one word that would give her hope. Dragging her feet, she was jostled by the hurrying crowd. A rattling baggage cart ran over the end of her skirt. Was that Foy she saw?

The conductor lifted her elbow, propelling her aboard.

Hands and nose pressed to the window, she peered out. Joyfully she saw that it was Foy striding toward her! Behind him a dark head—Mignonne? No, Lily. Suddenly he stopped. Adrianna arose. With a great screeching, the train jerked forward. Slamming into the unyielding seat, she cried out in pain. Tears unleashed, she peered again through the vibrating window. She saw Foy growing ever smaller, arm held high, waving goodbye.

six

Foy banged his fist against the baggage cart. "What an idiot I've been," he growled. Shaking his smarting hand, he looked despairingly after the train.

Lily stood quietly beside him until the roar and rattle subsided. With warm sympathy in her eyes, she replied, "Yes, little brother, I'm afraid so. Tell me, now, why did we come to see Adrianna off and not speak to her?"

"I don't know," Foy said miserably. He plunged both hands into his sun-streaked hair. "I've never felt so . . ." He let out a disgusted snort, and his voice deepened reflectively. "From the moment I looked down at that blazing red hair and saw her walking down the street into danger . . ." His ears reddened and he grinned ruefully. "I'll admit I was smitten." He shrugged. "But then I realized I'm way too old for her. It's best she's gone."

Foy grasped Lily's elbow to guide her through the bustling depot, but she stood firmly. "You're not that old, Foy. You just never had a chance to be young. You were a child when you went off to war. It was seeing so many men die that makes you feel—Foy, you didn't let Adrianna go without telling her you love her?"

Foy groaned noncommittally. "But do I? One minute she's so warm, so full of humor." He turned from Lily. "Then she slips away into—" He lifted tense shoulders in puzzlement then dropped them in defeat. "I can't tell what she's thinking. I want to believe she feels what I feel. But then she turns a smile on Green that would melt an avalanche."

"She loves you," said Lily with conviction. She laughed

lightly. "I was beginning to think my baby brother would never fall in love."

"Yeah." He ducked his head. "I'd steeled myself against the local belles. I can't afford to get married. Not with every penny tied up building the *Mignonne*."

"I know." Lily sighed and patted his arm. "And I'm sorry about the confusion over Mignonne. To us she's still a child. It's time we realized."

"I thought I was doing the right thing taking her along." Foy smoothed his wild hair. "Thought I was providing a proper chaperone, but Adrianna's probably too worldly to—"

"No, I doubt that."

"You like her, then?" Foy looked at Lily eagerly. "I was afraid you—she's been raised so differently."

Lily laughed delightedly. "Of course I do. You know I love people for the good I see in them. The poor child's been spoiled and confused. Anyone who had to live with that Isadora Atherton . . ." Lily's voice became an icy hiss.

Foy chuckled. "Still jealous!" He wagged a teasing finger, then sobered. "I suppose it doesn't matter what we think. Adrianna's so wealthy and I . . . Sister, I can't even afford her fancy French perfume!"

"What she needs is love she can count on, love that won't be snatched away," said Lily sadly. "She has a natural joie de vivre that I found charming, but the loneliness in her eyes hints that she's never found the joy of committing her life to the Lord. I'd welcome the opportunity to counsel her. You know how strongly I feel that a Christian should marry a person who is Christian if the marriage is to have a lasting foundation."

Silently they walked out of the noisy depot.

Foy made a harsh, sorrowful sound. "You want to save her soul and I want . . ." He shook his head disgustedly. "We let our chance go by. The one love of my life, and I'll never see her again!"

Pacing the deck of the *Mignonne Wingate*, Foy tortured himself for all the things he could have said. He had let Green Bethune's wealth diminish him to the speechless anger he had felt sixteen years earlier when Green had tried to captivate Lily. Witty words crowded Foy's mind now that it was too late.

He crossed the freight deck and stepped down into the engine room where workmen stood laughing and talking.

"Hey boys, we've got to get these boilers installed." Foy tried to push pleasantly. If the steamboat had been more nearly completed, he would have felt freer to offer Adrianna his love.

Frustrated at the slow progress, Foy climbed to the pilot-house. He gripped the seven-foot wooden steering wheel until his knuckles whitened. Foy had longed to be a river pilot from the moment Captain Harrison Wingate had fired his twelve-year-old enthusiasm with the challenges of unexpected adventure on the river. Even the boiler explosion on the gunboat *Chattahoochee* had not shattered his dream. Because Jonathan Ramsey's wound sustained in the disaster had led to the amputation of his foot, Foy felt pleased to give him the job of managing the Edwardses' Cotton Exchange.

Free to follow his dream, Foy had learned the pilot's craft at the hand of a master, Bose Marcrum. Eager, intense, Foy had advanced quickly from the apprenticeship known on this river as a striker pilot. For top certification he had been required to draw from memory a detailed map of the river from Columbus to Apalachicola Bay. Now he looked with pride at the wall where he had hung his license.

He was ready to live his dream. If only the workmen would keep the hammers banging. Frustrated, he plunged his fingers into his hair. *And still the river needs clearing*!

Sighing deeply, Foy seemed to smell the lingering scent of hyacinths in the small enclosure. His brows drew down in a frown. *Could this life ever make a sophisticated woman like Adrianna content*?

Sometimes Adrianna seemed so happy. Her voice sounded like a smile. Suddenly he remembered its painful tone as she confessed her lie. "I had to get away," she had said, "loving you . . ." Loving you! He leaned his head against the wheel and groaned. With nothing to offer her, he had left her precious words floating between them, unanswered.

Disgusted with himself, Foy pounded his fist against the wheel. *Then that bragging idiot Green oiled his way between us like he did Lily and Harrison*!

Distraught, Foy stamped down to the grand saloon where the mahogany dance floor had just been finished. Throwing aside his coat and rolling up his sleeves, he dropped to his knees and briskly rubbed in beeswax.

Exhausted by bedtime, Foy felt calmer. He wrote a long, ink-stained letter to Adrianna pouring out his desire to marry her when he could become established. Satisfied, he fell asleep. At midnight, he awakened and ripped the letter to shreds. At two o'clock he wrote a careful, chatty letter, merely signing it, "I love you." At daybreak, he realized he could not mail it. He did not know where Adrianna had gone.

Lily passed breakfast ham to a downcast Foy. "Senator Atherton and Isadora have returned to Washington," she said.

Harrison looked at him seriously. "The Senator's arranging for us to testify at a hearing. He feels certain the time is right for a Congressional appropriation to clear the channel."

'Y'all go," Foy mumbled without looking up. "I'll stay and

try to push some work out of the men."

"You might need this while we're gone," Lily added.

Foy unfolded the paper she thrust into his hand and read the Madison, Georgia, address of Adrianna's mother. He grinned at his sister. Lily never moped and moaned. She made things happen.

After posting his letter, Foy threw himself into work with a fury. Daily his hopes rose at mail time. Daily he was disappointed.

On the eighteenth of December, a telegram came. Fearful that some mishap had befallen Adrianna, Foy ripped it open.

FIRE. WAREHOUSE TEN. 750 BALES LOST. COME.

JONATHAN

Foy moaned. Dangling his hands between his knees, he sat staring into space. That warehouse had been his insurance against disaster.

Throughout the journey back to Eufaula, Foy berated himself. Perhaps he should decide if he were a cotton factor or a river pilot. Should he stay behind his father's old desk and be ready to take advantage of the constantly fluctuating market instead of following his dream of the river?

When he reached home and came in sight of the Cotton Exchange, Foy's shoulders lifted and his chest swelled with pride. He would not let the frustration Green had caused sway him from his goal. He would remain a cotton broker, buying bales from the farmers. One day he would be more than just the middle man. He would also own the river packets on which the bales were taken to Apalachicola Bay to be transferred to ocean-going vessels bound for the cotton mills of Lancashire. Determined, Foy strode into his father's old office.

Jonathan sat slumped behind the enormous desk. Seeing Foy, he said bitterly, "I've failed you boy!"

"Nonsense! What happened?"

"I thought if J.G. Guice could come back from the war with his good right arm gone and become one of the South's best samplers and graders of cotton, that surely I . . ." He wiped his red nose. "I'm no good as a cotton factor. Maybe the Lord is trying to tell me something!"

"Fires happen. You know how often cotton will catch fire at the gin and smolder from the inside of the bale for weeks before air strikes and it flames."

"Yes . . ." Jonathan blew his nose and struggled to control his emotions. "That's what most folks tell you, but . . ."

"Did you try soapy water? It will penetrate when plain water will roll off."

"With this fire we didn't have a chance. Come on. You might as well see for yourself."

The distinctive smell of burning rags assailed Foy's nose long before he turned the corner and saw Warehouse Ten, a pile of still smoldering wreckage.

"Whew!" Foy whistled between his teeth. He had known the cotton would be damaged, but he had hoped to sell some for salvage. Every bale was completely gone.

"Every able-bodied man in town was passing buckets," said Jonathan. "The E.B. Youngs got here with their hand engine. The best they could do was save the other buildings. I've never seen such a flash fire. Bales were blazing!"

Foy began to kick the charred remains.

"Could have been the weather," Jonathan mused. "It was one of those drastic changes, hot one day, then extremely cold, sleeting like everything. The cotton froze."

Foy leaned over a blackened corner post and sniffed. "Coal oil!"

"Expanded," Jonathan continued, "burst a steel band. It could have struck a spark, started a fire in the jute bagging."

"Not this time." Foy knelt to smell a brick pillar.

"You're right, Foy." A deep voice intervened.

Foy turned and nodded grimly to Dan Rowlett.

"I told the boys when we were fighting the fire, 'Boys,' I said, 'this don't look right to me.'"

"Arson?" Jonathan gasped.

Rowlett's head jerked curtly. "Fire was blazing from three different spots."

"Who?" asked Foy.

"I've got me ideas," Rowlett answered, "but I can't prove a thing."

"Well, Jonathan," Foy said with false heartiness as he clapped the distraught man's shoulder, "it's my fault. Not yours. Every carpetbagger and scalawag in town knows my part in the Keils affair. They are out to get me!"

On Christmas Eve in somber spirits, Foy picked up his gun and whistled for his dog. He set out on his annual tramp through the woods in search of game for Emma's Christmas dinner. He missed Harrison, who had not returned from Washington, and Jonathan, who could not hike with his artificial limb.

Usually Foy felt at peace in the freedom of nature, but after an hour, his game bag remained empty. His tension increased as he stepped into a clearing and surveyed abandoned fields. Once green acres were choked with vines and scrub.

Adrianna is just too young, he thought. *A mere child when the war ended, she could not understand the devastation.*

Even after the armistice had been signed, General

Grierson's men had seized horses and livestock at will while scouring the country looking for Jefferson Davis. After the Confederate President was taken prisoner, the war seemed really over and weary soldiers plodded home. How galling it had been to watch Federal Guards stop proud men and force them to show paroles before they could cross the covered bridge which spanned the Chattahoochee.

How doggedly they fought for their homes and their belief in the inalienable right of local self-government, Foy thought. He was proud that Alabama had contributed 122,000 soldiers to the Confederate Army, saddened that 35,000 fell before the musket and disease. Foy had returned from naval duty to a Eufaula filled with wounded and dying men. With capital gone and labor scattered, the returning heroes were subjected to Federal Occupation troops and disfranchisement.

Getting rid of Keils will help, Foy thought. *We can snap back with a little more time. Time! Will Adrianna wait?*

Looking as if through Adrianna's eyes at a once palatial mansion, unpainted, crumbling, he wondered how he could ask her to wait. His farmer friends, small and great alike, struggled to maintain themselves by planting meager patches instead of great fields of cotton.

How had Green maintained his wealth? I can't compete with him.

Trudging down a muddy lane, Foy reached a crossroad and entered a frame building. Speaking to a group of men heatedly discussing farming and politics, Foy stretched cold hands toward the potbellied stove. Dipping his hand into a big wooden barrel for a dry cracker, he overheard a once-proud matron bartering eggs.

"Oh, you must make it one more orange," she pleaded. "One for each child's stocking." Softly under her breath, she added, "It's all they will have for Christmas."

Foy's fingers separated the few coins in his pocket. He must leave one each for Kitty and Lige who seemed not to realize that Christmas would never be the same. They still awakened him with shouts of, "Chris'mus gif', I seed you first!"

Stepping around an open tub of corned mackerel, Foy ducked back and grinned as a brown stream of tobacco juice barely missed him. He looked over his head. At least the stores had Christmas merchandise again. Toys were suspended from the ceiling among the lanterns, horse collars, and buggy whips. He moved to where a huge bag was spilling out rough brown coconuts. Since boyhood, it had been his job to ceremoniously place a nail in the eye of a Christmas coconut and hammer a well placed blow. He would drain the thin, white milk and drink it before he whacked the coconut to split it. How juicy were those first morsels Emma grated for her special cake!

Happily, Foy selected a perfect coconut and a hoop of ripe-smelling cheese for Emma and Jonathan. Feeling certain that Lily would not miss Christmas at home, he bought Brazil nuts and Malaga grapes for her and Harrison and rock candy for Mignonne. Foy then turned to the counter where a wooden box lined with red paper seemed to draw him. Excitedly, Foy rummaged among the Chinese firecrackers for the ones which would make the most noise. For Harrison Junior he picked a torpedo. Beau was at the age to enjoy slipping up on a group of girls and throwing it at their feet to make them squeal. For Emma and Jonathan's son, Wingate Ramsey, Foy bought a Roman candle. It would light up the heavens with its fiery balls and delight Win's eight-year-old heart.

Whistling as he left the country store, Foy almost missed the covey of quail flushed by his bird dog. Bagging one Bob White, he became more watchful.

Stepping softly over a carpet of pine needles and leaf mold, Foy was swallowed into the dark forest. Sunlight broke through on the top of a poplar turning it to shimmering gold. Suddenly a deer leaped, bounding over the path with her white tail flagging. She disappeared into the undergrowth. All was quiet, at peace.

The sharp-scented air cleared his thinking. A worshipful feeling of God here with him filled his being.

"Thank You, God, for creating such beauty," Foy prayed.

"Thank You that my war wounds are healed and I have strength to forge ahead. Help me to know if Adrianna is the wife You've chosen for me."

Adrianna. Her name seemed to float tantalizingly beyond the next turning. His feeling for her had exploded so intensely, so suddenly that he had tried to dismiss it as infatuation. Picking up a purple sweet gum leaf, he smoothed the starlike surface and knew that the longing he felt was love. He gathered some of the hard, prickly burs. Would Adrianna ever like anything so simple as dipping sweet gum burs in silver paint to decorate for Christmas?

A turkey mounted up before him on strong wings. Foy cupped his hand around his mouth and called, "Gobble-gobble-gobble."

"Gobble-gobble." The wizened head of another turkey popped from behind a bush.

Bang!

My luck is changing, Foy exulted as he picked up the heavy turkey. Even wild game had been scarce since the war.

Striding back through Eufaula toward the Ramsey's small, homey cottage, Foy rounded the corner. Just as he had anticipated, the Wingates had arrived.

"Christmas!" Lily shouted as she ran toward him with

arms outstretched.

Harrison clapped him on the shoulder. "Great news! Washington says the Chattahoochee channel will be cleared!"

When they all went to church on Christmas morning, the world seemed right again save for Foy's wistful dreams of Adrianna's bright red head added to the family circle.

On the coldest day of January, it arrived: a letter which smelled of springtime.

> *Abington Hotel*
> *New York City, New York*
> *January 20, 1875*

Dear Mr. Edwards:

I shudder to know what you must think of me for being such a tardy correspondent, but your letter followed me from Georgia to Washington, where I stayed only briefly before my grandfather sent me to New York to further my education. Your nice letter finally caught up with me here.

I'm afraid I must have appeared an empty-headed ninny among all you purposeful people. I'm studying philosophy to help get my feelings more properly controlled by reason.

Don't you find all these modern ideas like Darwin's exciting? Next I might study art.

I spent my first Christmas with snow. It was lucky that Grandfather and Ma-ma's present was a warm fur because I enjoyed walking the snowy streets. The city was bustling with shoppers buying elegant gifts. The lights were bright and the music gay. But don't you find sometimes one gets lonely in a crowd?

Please write and tell me all about your new

steamer. I promise to answer quickly this time.

Your friend,
Adrianna Atherton

Foy held the letter against his face and breathed its sweet fragrance. *Lily is right,* he thought. *Wealth and furs don't warm the heart.* Closing his eyes, he could picture Adrianna's face bubbling with cheerfulness, then becoming wistful when she thought no one was watching.

How he longed to gather her in his arms, to kiss her, to show her she was loved! With an ache in his throat, he took out his leather writing case and carefully composed a letter telling her that work was to begin on clearing the river. "The *Mignonne* is almost finished," he wrote. "I can't wait for you to see her."

Foy sat back and wiped sweaty palms. Could she read between the lines his desire for her to share his life? As yet he dared not declare his love.

Adrianna's reply came quickly. Chatty, the letter held no clue to her feelings for him. Foy puzzled over a passage about art:

> *The first Impressionist exhibition in Paris last fall was laughed at as a grotesque bohemian joke, but some of my American friends are assimilating it into "luminism." I like their use of a blonde palette and long to go to Paris to see this new work of Claude Monet and Auguste Renoir.*

Panic-stricken, Foy feared that Adrianna would go to France and be lost to him forever. He wrote back immediately:

> *I don't understand a word you are saying about art, but I'm proud of your growing talent. Darling, please don't*

go to Paris. Couldn't you paint the flowers in Eufaula?

Exhausted from long, trying hours at work, Foy relaxed by writing to Adrianna before he went to bed. The letters often took several nights to finish. Her long, sweet replies and the interest she took in things that mattered to him delighted him. He felt she had gone astray on philosophy when she wrote:

> *The new currents of thought coupled with technological and industrial advances have everyone questioning old values and searching for new means of adapting to the rapid changes in the economic and social environment. I'm interested in the new pragmatism. It is so much easier to live with than the old idealism.*

They argued through several letters. She thought he was dogmatic in his assertion of the unchanging principles of the Bible.

In spite of these disagreements, the chain of letters spanned the distance through the early summer and forged a bond of friendship. Their first infatuation deepened into love as they learned more about each other, but each feared to reveal their feelings.

Columbus, Georgia
July 15, 1875

> *The* Mignonne *should be finished in two weeks! The stained-glass windows have been installed and I can't wait for you to see them.*

Foy sat, pen poised. Now he was ready to declare his love, ask her to return. As he hesitated, a hot west wind warned him to wait. It signaled disaster.

Drought!

The burning wind continued. The sun scorched everything green into brittle, lifeless brown. Each afternoon, temperatures reached 100, 105, 110 degrees. Strong men collapsed, even died.

> *Eufaula, Alabama*
> *August 21, 1875*

Dear Adrianna,

> *There are no beautiful cotton fields for you to paint. The plants stand stalwartly surviving, but without rain, they produce no fluffy white bolls, only useless stalks to be mowed down.*

> *I thought I was building two empires, but both of them were dependent on cotton. Cotton and weather. Even if I had a load to haul, we couldn't get the Mignonne out of Columbus. The drought has nearly dried up the lakes and rivers.*

Putting down his pen and pacing his room, Foy wondered if he should try to explain that he had no money to ask her to marry him. No. He banged one fist against the other. City people never understood why farmers could suddenly be overwhelmed by debts through no fault of their own. Could he make Adrianna understand that the economy of the whole region was tied to agriculture?

He dipped his pen in the ink and shook his head sadly as he finished his letter without a proposal:

> *At least the low water helps efforts to clear the channel of the Chattahoochee.*

> *I love you,*
> *Foy*

Eufaula, Alabama
October 2, 1875

The rains came too late. There were no spring or summer crops. The farmers are doggedly saying next year will be better and are preparing to plant for winter.

At least the political drought seems over. I can see Reconstruction coming to a close and Eufaula becoming safe for young brides again. With the Radical Party in control and Elias Keils giving safe asylum to thieves, we have lived in constant danger.

You'll be happy to know that Keils has fled the state. A new constitution this year will spread the voting to precincts. There should be no more riots, but then you do meet exciting people during riots, don't you?

Only the threat of fire remains. Some are natural from city growth, but some are still being set.

Foy's confidence improved when the price of his stored cotton went up again. Joyfully he paid his bills and settled old debts.

Eufaula, Alabama
November 4, 1875

My Darling Adrianna,

I can't believe it's been a year since the wonderful day we met. It seems like yesterday, yet like forever, and I long to see you! I'm sending you a Christmas present. I hope your family will feel I have courted you long enough for you to accept. I am only waiting now for the river to rise.

Winter rains drenched the mountains, and once again the Chattahoochee became a mighty river hurrying to the sea. The family returned to Columbus for final work on the *Mignonne*.

Foy began a letter which would be his carefully rehearsed marriage proposal.

> *Columbus, Georgia*
> *January 5, 1876*
>
> *The* Mignonne *is afloat! We've taken her on a few runs to try her machinery. She's ready . . .*

A brisk knock sounded at his door and Lily burst into the room.

"Guess what?" she exclaimed, waving two letters under his nose. "The Cleburne Fire Company wants to hire the *Mignonne Wingate*. They plan to raise money for a new engine by selling tickets for a spring charity excursion to Apalachicola Bay. It'll be a grand occasion! We'll be filled to capacity. Oh, Foy!" She regarded him with liquid brown eyes. "This is the beginning!"

"How about inviting Senator and Mrs. Atherton and honoring them since he got Congress to clear the channel?"

"And Adrianna?" Lily teased.

"And Adrianna, of course!"

"This other letter is from her." Lily gave him a hug as she left the room."

Eager to write his letter, Foy scanned Adrianna's words inattentively until she mentioned one man's name.

> *I'm not as lonely now. I've been seeing the latest plays and all the sights, including the new Brooklyn Bridge. You'll never guess who looked me up. That nice man you all introduced me to, Mr. Green Bethune.*

Foy crushed the letter and hurled it savagely at the wall.

seven

Adrianna wandered aimlessly down the crowded New York street through swirling April Fool's Day snow. Snowflakes clinging to her eyelashes merged with tears as she agonized, *Have I done the wrong thing again? No*, she thought, *I should not have written Foy about Green.*

Sighing, she shrugged her fur-trimmed jacket more tightly about her neck. She should have been satisfied with their growing friendship, but every time she had felt Foy's letters warming to love, he had seemed to draw back. How foolish she had been to think she could push him into proposing by using Green to make him jealous. She must have hurt him— or angered him. He had not replied.

Turning into the wind, Adrianna trudged toward her hotel. At first, winter in the city had exhilarated her senses, but now she longed for the warmth and perfumed flowers of the South as much as she ached to feel Foy's arms.

"Well, not quite as much," she whispered to herself, giggling.

Adrianna had been closely supervised in New York yet lonely. She had remained on the edges of the sophisticated groups who avidly discussed the confusing new theories for living lives of self-gratification.

Then without warning, Green Bethune had appeared at her hotel. He had presented her with an insurance policy paid for by Isadora. Adrianna had started to turn away, but her homesickness responded to the soft southern sound of his voice. She had eagerly accepted when he invited her to dinner and the theater. The charming man had made certain that the cuisine was superb, the play witty and intelligent.

Adrianna had settled easily into being squired about town. Green had showered her with attention and would fit well into the political arena that was her family's life. Even though she had fallen more in love with Foy with each letter from him, she must be realistic. It was time to admit that he had made no commitment. She must forget Foy and decide on Green.

With her chin high, Adrianna entered the Abington and walked past the hotel desk. It had been so long since she wrote Foy, hoping to push him into a proposal of marriage by making him jealous of Green, that she was beginning to realize he must be too angry to reply.

Her dimpled chin trembled. Yes, this was one more time she had been wrong. She gritted her teeth. Didn't one of the philosophies she was studying say it was all right to do the wrong thing for the right reason? But was it?

At the elevator, Adrianna turned back to inquire for messages. The desk clerk handed her a letter. Ripping it open, she let her eyes dance over the words.

> *Eufaula, Alabama*
> *March 3, 1876*
>
> *The Mignonne is afloat! We've taken her on a few runs to try her machinery. She's ready! We've made some freight hauls, but her formal introduction into service will be a grand excursion trip to the bay as a charity fund raiser for the Cleburne Fire Company. We are inviting Senator and Mrs. Atherton, and I hope very much that you can be here April twenty-seventh.*
>
> *Your friend,*
> *Foy Edwards*

Her delight burst radiantly upon the dazzled clerk. "Get my

bill ready, please," she said. "I'm going . . ." Adrianna paused. How could she explain? Then the word rang out with certainty: "Home!"

The crashing of cymbals and the oom-pa-pa of a tuba underscoring a lively brass band echoed up Eufaula's bluff as Adrianna's carriage descended toward the riverside. The *Mignonne Wingate* floated regally, dazzling white against the dark Chattahoochee. The music was coming from the hurricane deck where a big bass drum was emblazoned with the name, *Professor Ryan's Sunny South Brass Band*. Crowds of people milled about laughing, calling greetings.

Adrianna's breath caught in her throat. She clasped her fingertips over her open mouth in sudden fear of her long-anticipated meeting with Foy. She swept the passengers with appraising eyes. Self-confident ladies, every inch as stylish as those on the streets of New York, promenaded in lavishly draped bustles of every hue. The men wore jackets of muted blacks, browns, and blues. Most of them had given up the old-fashioned high top hats and replaced them with the new round hard ones.

Sighing, Adrianna wished she had anticipated the crowd and written Foy which train to meet. In her excitement about seeing him, she had not considered how formal his invitation had been. Adrianna fought tears. Perhaps Foy simply wanted to add her to the crowd.

Should I go back? she wondered. *Have I come only to break my heart?*

Wiping a tear, she lifted her eyes to the pilothouse. Foy! Arm straight up, he waved frantically, then bounded down endless flights of stairs.

There is some use to red hair, she thought, giggling nervously as she slipped and slid down the hill.

Foy's feet hit the gangplank in three rocking bounces that threatened to tumble him into the water. "You came," he shouted. "You're alone!" It was a joyful cry.

"Yes." Adrianna stopped, waiting as he scrambled up the slope. Puzzled by his intensity, she asked, "Aren't my grandparents here?"

"No, they . . ." Foy stopped short. "I was afraid." His brows came together and a muscle twitched in his set jaw. "I didn't know whether to invite you or not. Mrs. Atherton was frightened of the river. I debated a long time."

Adrianna's sensitive face paled and her lip trembled. Tension crackled between them. She searched his scowling countenance with troubled eyes.

"I was afraid," he repeated low in his throat, "that you might bring Green!"

"No!" Adrianna gasped. "Oh, Foy, I shouldn't have teased. I wanted to make you—" She lifted her hand toward his face and leaned yearningly closer. "I hoped you'd invite me back." She snapped her fingers and said, "I don't care that for Green."

Foy laughed in relief. Looking at her hungrily, he stepped as close as he dared and whispered, "You are more beautiful than my dreams." He breathed deeply and rolled his eyes heavenward.

Adrianna's laughter rang out as she watched him react to the warm waft of her perfume. Love was plain on his tender face. How she regretted that she had hurt him! She longed to fling herself into his arms, yet even if they had been betrothed, decorum permitted no such public display.

Meeting his eyes, she said lightly, "Hello, I'm Adrianna Atherton."

"Foy Edwards, Esquire." He grinned and tipped his pilot's cap. Proffering his elbow, he escorted her across the gangway.

"May I present the grandest steamboat on the Chattahoochee, the *Mignonne Wingate*. She is named, of course, for my partner's daughter."

Adrianna laughed ruefully. As they reached the lower deck and were sheltered slightly from curious eyes, she said, "Oh, Foy, you look so . . ." She swallowed her flooding emotions. "Wonderful! So tanned and strong." Her bare ring finger lightly tapped his hard-muscled arm and her eyes caressed his high cheekbones. "So confident."

"You've changed." Foy laughed huskily. "You're exquisite!"

Foy's dark eyes devoured the perfection of her trim figure encased in the slim column of white silk. Wonderingly, he brushed the back of his hand against her cheek which had lost some of its roundness.

"Have you been eating enough?"

"Just lost my baby fat." She laughed again, pleased at the impact she had made upon him. "Foy, I'm sorry that—"

Uhmmmmm! Uhmmmmm!

The growling blast of the whistle made her jump. Shattering their private moment, the sound signaled a final flurry of activity. Uhmmmmm! Uhmmmmm! Echoes bounced from bank to bank. Chanting more quickly, the deckhands reached for the last of the freight from the sweating men who had carried it down the steep bluff. With a shout, the shoreman lifted the loop of heavy rope from the post and tossed it to the deck. The whistle kept blasting as the gangplank folded upward. The great paddle wheel at the stern shuddered. Turning slowly, it churned a white wake.

Foy was swept away by a call. Across the crowd of passengers, Adrianna sought him with her eyes. They exchanged wordless promises for later.

Warmed, ecstatically happy, Adrianna turned to find Lily at

her side. Foy's sister introduced her to several people. Then she showed her to her private stateroom.

Glad Foy had not assigned her a berth in the ladies' sleeping cabin, Adrianna retreated gratefully. Stretching luxuriously on her bed, she savored each moment of meeting Foy. Mentally, she kissed his straight nose, the heavy brows which shielded his smoldering eyes, his hollow cheeks, his lips. Shivering with delight at her dreaming, Adrianna was glad she had dismissed Mrs. Cristie when she stopped at the hotel to rest and change.

From Foy's invitation, she had expected her grandparents to be along. She had thought she would be amply chaperoned. Biting her lip, she hoped no one would gossip that she was traveling alone, but she did enjoy solitude. She felt suddenly shy.

Changing to a demure, billowy pink cotton set off by lace and wine velvet bows, Adrianna picked up her sketchbook. Determinedly, she stepped out into the warm April sunshine.

She seated herself on deck and was immediately struck by the solitary feeling of a dead pine clinging to the bank. She tried to capture the emotion of the scene with charcoal.

Suddenly Foy was bending over her, nodding approvingly. He said, "Ready for your tour?"

Adrianna smiled and followed him down to the lower deck past freight neatly stacked and bales of cotton on which the deckhands lounged. Foy guided her closer to the big boilers and the steam engine which turned the paddle wheel. Grimacing, she put her hands over her ears against the roar as firemen fed the hungry firebox under the boiler with long sticks of cordwood.

They climbed back to the elegant grandeur of the upper deck and leaned over the rail to let the spring breeze cool their cheeks. Adrianna's eyes sparkled with excitement as she said fervently, "The *Mignonne*'s a beautiful boat."

"Isn't she?" Foy grinned. "She's as slim and restive as a

thoroughbred race horse."

Proudly, Foy showed her through the inviting lounge. Next they peeped into the dining room. White-uniformed waiters were setting tables covered in immaculate linen.

"We'd better hurry," said Foy. They sniffed at the spicy odors already filling the room and their mouths watered.

Grasping Adrianna's elbow, Foy helped her up the steps to the hurricane deck where he tapped on the door of the captain's office.

Harrison Wingate welcomed the smiling pair. The rich, dark woods in the room were set off by gleaming brass. "We're pleased you've joined us, Miss Adrianna. Seems as though April 27, 1876, will be a banner day for the Wingates and the Edwards."

"I'm delighted to be part of your first excursion, Captain Wingate," Adrianna replied warmly. "It certainly is a success."

"Yes," he agreed. "The Cleburne Fire Company turned out in full force."

"Firemen?" Adrianna queried. "So refined, so elegantly dressed?"

"They are the cream of Eufaula society." Harrison laughed at her astonishment.

"The volunteer firemen," Foy explained, "are the leading men of the town. They're organized to protect their homes. We have several different companies. They practice precision drills, sort of like the old militia groups."

"Are there still so many fires?" asked Adrianna.

"Bad fires average one every six weeks," replied Harrison gravely. "Some are a natural result of congested city growth, but many are set by arsonists. In 1872, whole blocks of our business district burned."

"Things are better since Dan Rowlett became chief of the Eufaula Fire Department," said Foy. "They have one hook and ladder company and there are two hand engines, but we need more. The Cleburne Company put on this charity excursion to raise money for an engine and a firehouse. I must introduce you to the ladies who planned it, Mrs. G.L. Guice and Mrs. Wells Bray. You'll especially like Miss Islay Reeves. With all their enthusiastic work, we'll soon have better fire protection."

The happy couple continued their tour of the steamer by looking in quickly on Lily. Since she was already laying out evening clothes, they scampered up the stairs to the pilot-house. Foy introduced Adrianna.

"This is our pilot, Mr. Trimmer, and his striker, Ben."

Friendly, but with unmistakable arrogance, Trimmer let Adrianna watch. The big boat yielded to the slightest turn of the large steering wheel and followed the main channel safely around a bend.

From his spot on the lazy bench, Ben, the young apprentice steersman, gaped at Adrianna. Foy grinned smugly and squeezed a possessive arm around her shoulders as he helped her down from the pilothouse.

That evening when Adrianna stepped into the dining room, she remembered the gawky lad and wondered if the boat were safe in his hands. She saw the arrogant pilot in a corner, and Foy was striding toward her.

Adrianna's red hair danced on her bare shoulders and floated down the back of her elegant, pink satin gown.

Foy's deep-set eyes widened in delight as he drank in her appearance. He proudly offered his arm to escort her to the Captain's table.

Harrison Wingate was the image of quiet dignity in his dark

blue serge suit with brass buttons. Foy's navy blue uniform was less grand. The men guests wore dinner jackets and black ties. The ladies wore ornate gowns and jewels. Adrianna noticed Lily's emeralds, but what astonished her was Emma Ramsey. Seated at the next table, Emma moved in a pink glow from a huge ring and an elaborate necklace of rubies.

Relaxed, happier than she could ever remember, Adrianna enjoyed each course proffered by waiters in spotless white uniforms. She felt much more at ease than she had on her first visit.

"Everyone in New York," she said enthusiastically, "is discussing Charles Darwin's latest book, *The Descent of Man*, and debating his theory of evolution."

The table fell silent. Lily scowled. She had opened her mouth to retort when her son's high-pitched young voice brought an embarrassed red spot to her cheeks.

"I'd like another piece of custard pie please," Beau called loudly to the waiter.

With a steady hand to his wife's scolding finger, Harrison quietly nodded to the waiter to bring the boys more pie. Chuckling, the handsome captain launched into a funny story of old days on the river.

Thankful that attention had been diverted from her attempt to flaunt her newfound knowledge, Adrianna retreated within herself. Too late, she realized that by introducing such a controversial subject at the dinner table, she had been as childishly rude as Beau. With the end of supper, Lily invited the passengers to the front deck to watch the sunset on the water. Some of them remained, impatiently waiting for tables to be cleared for cards. Not wanting to be caught in a game of whist, Adrianna looked about frantically for Foy.

Her seeking eyes spotted his strong profile etched against the flickering lamp light as he spoke earnestly with Mr. Trimmer.

He flashed her a smile and started across the crowded room.

"It's time for my watch," Foy said in his deep, serious voice.

"Oh." It was a small, defeated sound.

"Would you like to watch the sunset?"

Not wanting to encounter Lily, Adrianna started to shake her head.

Foy leaned closer and whispered, "From the pilothouse?"

"Yes!"

Giddily she climbed the stairs, feeling she was ascending to the turret of her fairy castle.

While Ben murmured to Foy of changes in the river, Adrianna smiled down at the darkening water. Clouds reflected against its black, mysterious depths. The trees seemed to stand on tiptoe on their separate shores and reach their arms toward each other in vain. The boat glided smoothly, silently down the stream. There was little sound save for the soft chu-choooo, chu-choooo of escaping steam.

"Oh, look how pretty!" Adrianna broke the silence. Pointing to a waterfall which leaped in joyous abandon to make its creek one with the river, she turned to share the beauty with Foy.

Tall, strong, Foy held the wheel with a light touch. Not taking his eyes from her to look where she pointed, Foy wrapped her in his warm gaze.

Adrianna's eyes swept the bench, the confines of the glassed tower. Ben was gone. They were alone, at last.

"Do you think that you could learn to love," Foy's voice broke huskily. "The river?"

"Yes," she whispered. "I already do . . ." She turned her back so that he could not read the hunger on her face. "Love your river."

"But, you do understand," he cupped her chin with strong fingers and turned her delicate face toward his eager gaze.

Trembling, Adrianna waited. She must chart her course more carefully this time.

"You understand—" Foy cleared his throat. "That the Chattahoochee's always plotting ten ways to kill a steamboat. Harrison and I want to rebuild his steamer line, and Jonathan . . ." Gently he drew her nearer as he searched her face with worried eyes. Clearing his throat again, he said eagerly, "Jonathan is getting the Cotton Exchange on its feet. You could restore Barbour Hall. It would always be home." His long arm dropped tentatively around her slender waist.

"I've never had a real home," she whispered close to his chest.

Foy's arm tightened. Smothering her against him, he buried his face in her flaming hair. "Oh, Adrianna, I love you. I never knew it was possible to love anyone so much! Or hurt so much," he said in an agonized voice. "You tortured me with thoughts of you with Green!"

Wriggling free, Adrianna looked up into his dear face. Twining her fingers in his sun-streaked hair, she pulled it playfully. "You ninny!" She laughed. "It's you I love!"

Lifting her lips, Adrianna met his kiss joyfully.

Kissing her with rising passion, Foy threw both arms around her, crushing her against him.

Scarcely able to breathe, Adrianna let her mind light upon one brightly glowing word: *Home*! she thought. *Now I have a home. It is in Foy's arms*. Someday she would tell him. For now her whole being must respond to the urgency of his kisses.

Plop! Plop! Plop! Whirring, flopping, the wheel spun madly out of control. Foy grabbed it, hauled it around frantically, too late. With a shuddering quiver, the *Mignonne* struck a hidden outcropping along the shore.

"Half-speed, Mr. Murphey," Foy said, leaning over the

speaking tube to instruct the engineer far below.

Gently, carefully, Foy urged the huge, flat-bottomed craft off her grounding. She grazed the reef, slid by, sailed on smoothly.

"Good grannies, that was close!" exclaimed Foy, wiping his forehead. He grinned sheepishly as a scowling Mr. Trimmer appeared at the top of the stairs.

They followed the sighing sounds of music to the grand saloon where Lewis' String Band was playing. Smiling, too filled with emotion to speak, Adrianna accepted Foy's hand and stepped onto the dance floor. In each other's arms, close in the only way propriety allowed, they waltzed to their inner music. When they were separated by the intricate figures of a cotillion, Adrianna smiled vaguely at her other partners. She seemed to breathe only when she rejoined Foy's arms.

When the dancing ended, Foy lingered at her stateroom door. Emma and Jonathan walked by casually but with the watchful eyes of chaperones. Foy brushed a kiss on her temple and whispered with a voice full of promise, "Tomorrow."

"Tomorrow!" Adrianna sighed happily.

Sunlight streaming through her cabin window bathed Adrianna in a rosy glow. "Home," she whispered and hugged herself, pretending she was in Foy's arms. Stretching dreamily, she savored the joy of being loved, then bounded out of bed anticipating a day with Foy.

Foy was nowhere to be seen at breakfast. Not daring to climb to the pilothouse, Adrianna decided to take her easel to the front of the boat. As she sat back, trying to capture the new techniques of Monet, Adrianna suddenly felt someone behind her.

Lily, her face clouded by an unaccustomed scowl, was bearing down upon her. "Adrianna," Lily snapped. "I simply must speak with you about last night!"

eight

Adrianna clapped her fingertips to her flaming cheeks, heedless of the paintbrush which scattered yellow oil across her dress.

"Yes, Miss Lily?" she replied meekly. Ducking her head, she dabbed at the flecks of paint and wondered, *Did Mr. Trimmer tell Captain Wingate my being in the pilothouse endangered the boat?* She lifted troubled eyes to the angry face of Foy's sister.

Lily was obviously struggling to control her temper. Pressing her lips together, she glanced at Adrianna's canvas. Distracted, she spoke in a strained voice. "Why, that's lovely! You've captured the light shimmering on the water in such a different way."

"It's a new technique," Adrianna replied warily. "You use pure color and try to capture the light and atmosphere, the sensation of the moment."

"I like it very much," Lily said.

Her frown deepened and again her voice was intense. "It's not that we here are against change, Adrianna. I've always fought against anyone saying that we must do something a certain way simply because we've always done it."

Adrianna's eyes darted about frantically. If only Foy would come to her rescue.

"Your mind has obviously been broadened by travel and study," Lily said. "But as hostess here, I must point out that one simply does not bring up anyone as controversial as Mr. Darwin at a social dinner table."

"Oh!" Adrianna's mouth remained round and she felt hot

and cold at the same time. "I'm sorry. I—" She had realized she was wrong, but something in Lily's tone made her jut her chin and speak defiantly. "I only meant to introduce stimulating conversation. I realize that for years these different theories of evolution have aroused tremendous conflict between science and religion. Even between Mr. Darwin and his wife and children, I've heard. But don't you think parts of the Bible are simply lovely myths?"

"Myths?" Lily exploded. "I certainly do *not*! Myths are fables written by people to explain gods. The Bible is God's Word written at His inspiration to reveal Himself to His people."

Hurt by Lily's dogmatic attitude, Adrianna became sarcastic. "Do you really believe all this," she said, waving her paintbrush at the passing woodland, "was created by God in only *seven* days?"

Foy's deep voice rumbled close behind her. "I do." He smiled warmly as she turned toward him, then he tenderly wiped a smudge of paint from her cheek. "But the Bible doesn't say twenty-four-hour days." His tone was gentle as he looked pleadingly from Adrianna to Lily. "Where does it say one day is with the Lord as a thousand years, and a thousand years as one day?"

"It's in Second Peter," replied Lily more evenly. "Peter was quoting Psalms and telling about creation and the end of the world."

Harrison, who had walked up with Foy, dropped a calming arm around his wife's tense shoulders and said, "It's the sudden surge in scientific thought that has fooled people into thinking they must choose either science or religion." Spreading his hands he continued in a quiet, firm voice. "Having spent much of my life alone with the stars, I know how unchangeable God is. As He reveals more to scientists, they will one day discover our world is larger and He is much greater than our little minds now grasp."

The angry churning of Adrianna's stomach was put to rest by Harrison's calming presence. Foy wrapped her in a loving glance, and she basked in the glow.

Lily had nodded agreement with her husband, but she persisted. "In the beginning, Darwin believed in God and was going to be a clergyman. I read that he said he did not in the least doubt the strict and literal truth of every word of the Bible. He himself never makes evolution a religious issue or takes part in all the silly debates that would make men monkeys. But," she flung out earnestly, "people are *not* brute beasts. God creates persons with *souls* to commune with Him."

"Darwin is beginning to leave God out as I once did." Emma's placid voice broke into their discussion.

Adrianna looked up in surprise as Emma and Jonathan joined their circle.

"I agree that God created man with a soul and made apes as separate creatures," Jonathan said. He began to chuckle. "Of course, you've gotta believe in some evolving when you see how much bigger this rascal's grown than our generation." Jonathan reached up to slap Foy's shoulders. Even Lily laughed.

Looking at each one in the loving group, Adrianna knew she wanted to become part of this family. Even in their slight differences of opinion, they could be understanding and supportive of one another.

"Seriously though," Jonathan continued. "It's not the question of evolution that matters, but if you place God first. Back in 1859, in his first edition of *Origin of the Species*, Darwin spoke frankly of God as Director of evolution. Sadly, his book was received with such enthusiasm by the German materialists that Darwin became intoxicated with his success. In the second edition, he cut God out."

Adrianna's conscience made her think for a moment that Jonathan was chiding her for becoming so impressed with her knowledge that she had left out God. Then she realized with some surprise that he was speaking of himself.

"We often start with faith," mused Jonathan. "But we end in folly because of our pride."

Passengers were filling the deck now. Some joined in discussions of the Social Darwinism that was sweeping the country. Others drifted away intent upon relaxing and forgetting cares.

Foy whispered close to Adrianna's ear, "Would you like to come to the pilothouse?"

Sparkling, she nodded and hurried to put away her paints.

Ben grinned as the laughing couple entered the pilothouse. Adrianna greeted the lanky boy pleasantly.

"Thought I'd starve afore yo' watch came.' Ben chuckled and gladly relinquished the wheel to Foy.

As soon as Ben's scruffy head disappeared, Foy said softly, "Come here."

Adrianna's rosy face glowed like sunlight on water as Foy's dark eyes enveloped her with his love. She moved into the shelter of his arms. Bending, he kissed her tenderly. He kept her close as he turned his attention to the wheel. Remaining nestled against him, she gazed at his strong, sharp profile as he peered at a distant point of land.

"If you'll be good," he said huskily, "and let me keep half a mind on my business, you can stay a while."

Adrianna's laughter tinkled. "I love it here," she said. "We're looking down on the world, and you are master of our fate."

"Well, God is master of our fate . . ."

Adrianna stiffened. Would Foy preach to her, too, or chide her about her argument with Lily?

"But," Foy continued. "He expects me to take serious responsibility for the lives of those on board, and today we'll be passing through the river's most dangerous parts."

Startled, Adrianna drew back a discreet distance. She thought of the people on the deck below pursuing pleasure with no thought of danger.

"How can you tell?" Adrianna asked. "Why, everything looks exactly the same."

Foy laughed. "No. Not really." He thought for a moment. "The main hazard is shallow spots, bars."

Adrianna nodded, remembering being stuck on the sandbar on the way to Columbus. Foy's serious tone reclaimed her attention.

"We're coming to a perilous spot none of us will ever forget, King's Rock. I was a kid, but I'll always remember that gray November day when Harrison wrecked." He shook his head reflectively. "Lily was waiting for Harrison to return for their wedding. There was a bad drought. The river was so low Harrison's boat, *Peytona*, smashed into King's Rock. Many lives were lost.

"We all gave up hope that Harrison had survived—except Lily," Foy continued. "Somehow, she knew Harrison was alive and would come to her. She has a strong belief in prayer and that God speaks to her to strengthen and guide." Foy fell silent, remembering.

"You really love your family, don't you?" Adrianna asked softly.

"Of course," Foy shrugged.

"I'm sorry I offended Lily. I'll try to be more careful. I want her to like me."

"She loves you," said Foy simply. Smiling down at her, he added, "We all do." His long arm hugged her rib-crushingly. Then he gently pushed her away and put both hands to the huge wheel.

Suddenly, the wide, gentle *Chattahoochee* funneled into a cut between walls of rock. The pent up water gushed forward striking hidden reefs. Foy's full attention was upon keeping the boat centered in the narrow passage. Wide-eyed, Adrianna nodded as he pointed out King's Rock. There had been no recent freshets, no mud to cloud the water. Today the water ran deep, and the flat-bottomed boat skimmed laughingly over the menacing rock.

Watching Foy steer carefully past, Adrianna wondered how much of a barrier Lily might be. Would Foy not ask her to marry him if Lily did not approve? She had hoped he might actually propose when she spoke of her longing for family, but now he was preoccupied and she knew she must be satisfied with his words of love and seeming assumption of a future marriage.

Piercing, unearthly cries made her jump. "What?" she mouthed as she clapped her hands over her ears. Foy could not hear her above the din. The wail ran up the scale like a human in distress. She could see that Foy was laughing.

"What in the world?" she asked when at last there was such silence that the surrounding woodland seemed to stop reeling and crouch in waiting.

"That demoniac yell," Foy said, laughing between words, "is the new steam whistle of the *Amos Hamilton*. Be glad you're not closer. She's coming down the Flint River trying to beat our schedule into the town of Chattahoochee."

"Well, I greatly prefer your whistle," Adrianna laughed, shivering.

"We'll be stopping for a while," Foy said. "We're in Florida now and some tourists always want to take a look at

the State Penitentiary." As he guided the steamboat to the
wharf, he spoke gruffly. "Many of my buddies died when
the *Chattahoochee*'s boiler exploded and she sank. I never
pass here without visiting their graves."

Adrianna felt good stretching her legs as she walked with a
silent Foy. When they reached the graveyard, she waited
quietly as he took off his cap and stood in sad contemplation.

" 'Oh! Susanna, oh don't you cry for me.' " Voices of
people lining the wharf raised to join the lively, if slightly off-
key, notes of a brass band playing from the hurricane deck of
the *Amos Hamilton*.

Adrianna's spirits lifted with excitement as another
whistle sounded. With flags flying, the *G. Gunby Jordan*,
floated smoothly to the wharf.

"She's the pride of the *People's Line*," Foy explained as
he took Adrianna's elbow and hurried her forward. "Com-
petition between the lines is becoming fierce."

Adrianna saw that a stream of people laden with picnic
baskets was hurrying to meet the *Jordan* while only a small
group approached the *Mignonne Wingate*.

"Oh, Foy!" Adrianna exclaimed. "They're taking all the
business!"

Foy laughed. "It's all right *this* time. Islay Reeves did such
a good job selling tickets to raise money for the fire engine that
we have a full load. But the *Wingate* Line is going to have to
scratch for a share of the trade. Fortunately, everyone likes
Harrison. The newspapers influence trade by the stories they
carry about how various captains manage their steamers."

Whistles were signaling departure.

Wheet! Wheet! The *G. Gunby Jordan* tooted impatiently,
lifted her gangplank, and sailed on.

Adrianna and Foy ran aboard their own boat and joined a party on the deck. Hours flitted by unnoticed. Isolated from the world, the boat drifted through flat, coastal plains forested in cottonwoods. The joyful plink, plink, plinking of a banjo set everyone's toes tapping as they listened to the well-known entertainer Matt O'Brien. They looked at each other in amazement as his small son, Master Marc, picked up a large guitar and began accompanying his father. Then father and son urged the whole group to join in singing popular songs.

Adrianna's voice rose happily as she sang, " 'Listen to the mockingbird, listen to the mockingbird, the mockingbird calling for its mate.' " She turned to smile meaningfully at Foy. He was watching the shoreline in tense-jawed silence.

"What's wrong?" she whispered, suddenly realizing the boat was moving slowly and turning frequently.

"Oh, nothing." Foy knit his brows and shook his head. "Just Moccasin Slough. It's a new channel caused by obstructions placed in the main river during the war."

"I thought the government had cleared . . ."

"They've improved it some, but it's still dangerous."

"Do you need to go to the pilothouse?" she asked half-fearfully, half-hopefully.

"No." Foy shook his head. "It's really shallow here. Old Trimmer says he's the only one who can take a steamboat over mud.' " He laughed and surveyed her with a warm gaze. "I hear the string band tuning up inside. It's still fifty miles to Apalachicola. Would you like to dance?"

"Of course!" Adrianna's eyes sparkled. "How long do we have?" she asked as they stepped onto the mahogany floor.

"Four hours," Foy said softly as he took her in his arms and breathed against her hair.

After the set, Adrianna and Foy went out to the deck to cool their faces. Adrianna noticed Lily and Harrison standing alone with their shoulders hunched in misery. Suddenly Harrison drew his wife into the shelter of his arms and kissed her. She sank forlornly against him.

Surprised because a public display of affection was considered improper, Adrianna looked at Foy questioningly. "Whatever is the matter?" she whispered.

Guiding her around the corner, Foy explained, "We're passing through the Narrows. During the war we had to block off the river to keep the enemy from attacking. This is where they sank the *Wave*."

Adrianna tried to understand. "The enemy sank—what?"

"No, no. Our navy sank several boats to obstruct the channel so that the Yankees could not sail upstream. Harrison and Lily had to sacrifice their steamer. They had fallen in love riding the *Wave*," he said softly. "The *Mignonne*'s dove insignia and the two longs of the whistle's signal belonged to the *Wave*."

Adrianna's eyes misted with understanding. She would never forget being in Foy's arms on his first boat. She peeped around the corner of the staterooms and saw Harrison tenderly cuff his wife's chin and whisper a laughing word to lift her spirits. Lily smiled wanly and wiped her tears.

Adrianna smudged a sympathetic tear and gazed up at Foy. "Now I understand a little more what the *Mignonne Wingate* means to you."

Foy rubbed his fingertip over her nose and chuckled.

"What? What?" she demanded stamping her foot.

"Since our walk this morning, you have six new freckles."

She made a wry face and tried to twist away.

"I want to kiss each one!" He bent nearer.

"Someone will see," she protested weakly as he kissed her cheekbone. She shivered deliciously as his kisses followed the spots dancing across the bridge of her nose.

Darkness had fallen by the time the *Mignonne* moored at the wharf in the town of Apalachicola. The next morning when Adrianna started out to breakfast, she was surprised to find everyone gathered at the rail chattering and exclaiming in dismay. Looking over Islay Reeves's head, Adrianna gaped at piles of brick and rubble, a scene of utter desolation.

"I was here two years ago," said Islay. "Then, it was the brightest, busiest, most prosperous city on the Florida coast. There were fine brick stores, expensive warehouses, elegant dwellings."

"What happened?" Adrianna gasped.

"The hurricane of 1874," Islay replied. "It did worse damage than the Yankees!"

For a moment the young women watched as supplies were loaded from the wharf; then, arm in arm, they went in and breakfasted on ham, eggs, grits, biscuits, and syrup. They barely noticed when the steamer left the mouth of the river to begin the cruise across Apalachicola Bay.

It was nine o'clock when Adrianna started down the central hallway to her stateroom. Suddenly she grabbed at her stomach which seemed to be falling to her toes. She lurched to the opposite side of the hallway. Her breakfast bounced as the boat rolled. Dismayed, she stumbled outside. Several ladies hung onto the rail, sea-sick.

The flat-bottomed river craft tossed giddily as ocean waves roughened Apalachicola Bay in spite of its protective chain of islands.

As the boat slowed and the choppiness calmed slightly, Adrianna adjusted to the pitch and yaw. Enraptured by the spectacular scenery, she gazed at the coastline of Florida. The beaches glittered white like poured out diamonds. The restless water sparkled like a brilliant aquamarine set in a ring of whitecaps.

Foy's strong brown fingers closed over her delicate hand. Seeming to sense her mood, he said nothing. They remained together as the steamer approached St. George's Island.

When the boat beached on a narrow slip of land, they walked two hundred yards across hard-packed wet sand to view the splendor of the Gulf of Mexico. Overwhelmed by the magnitude of the ocean, Adrianna felt her soul swelling out across the vastness. Reverence filled her as she remembered what Harrison had said. He was right. To have created this ocean, God was far greater than her mind had ever grasped.

"Would y'all like to go in bathing?" A timid voice broke her reverie.

Adrianna turned to see Mignonne standing shyly back.

"Oh, I'd love to." Adrianna's voice lifted with a smile. Eager to make amends with Foy's beautiful niece, she whispered companionably, "I brought the very latest bathing suit from New York."

"Mine is French," Mignonne confided.

Agreeing they would swim after lunch, Mignonne and Adrianna joined the ladies. They had exchanged their formal gowns for sportswear which differed from street clothes only in that the skirts did not drag on the ground. Adrianna blended happily in with the women and girls collecting shells.

Squeals of delight and cries of, "Come see the different shape of this one," or "Listen in this one for the sound of the ocean," wafted across the beach as the ladies filled their baskets. The small boys ran shouting in barefoot abandon, enjoying the freedom of one-piece, striped knit bathing suits.

Wondering where Foy had gone, Adrianna glanced up the

shore. The older men and women sat beneath canvas umbrellas. She laughed at the incongruity of the men in dark business suits and hats and the ladies in bonnets and blankets to protect them from the sun.

Suddenly she saw Foy smiling down upon her proudly. He had never looked more handsome. A blue silk scarf tie fluttered at his neck, and his light trousers and shirt were accented by a matching blue silk cummerbund. Foy waved a salute.

Adrianna tilted her head and beguilingly twirled her parasol. Foy strode forward purposefully as though ready at last to give her his undivided attention.

Strolling away from the crowd, they suddenly came to a stretch of beach completely covered with flat gray shapes.

"It looks as if a giant coin purse has spilled," said Adrianna.

"They are live sand dollars," Foy answered. He picked up one of the thin, flat sea urchins the size of a silver dollar. "God has made some wondrous creatures," he said. Turning it over, he rubbed off a bit of the velvet-like skin to show her the five-pointed pattern of holes for tube-feet.

"How can you tell it's alive?" Adrianna asked laughingly.

"Those are dead." Foy motioned to some of the wafers further up the shore which had bleached to bone-white. "Look closely at these," he said. "You can just see the hair-like particles moving."

Leaning closer, Adrianna cupped his hand to steady it, bringing it nearer. Her breath caught in her throat. "It's fascinating," she began. Open-mouthed, she looked up into his dark eyes. Shivering in the heat of his gaze, she waited, unmoving even though the warm Gulf waters rushed in around their feet. Gently Foy kissed her up-turned lips.

"Adrianna, my darling!" Foy's deep voice roughened with emotion as his arm came around her waist and he pulled her against his thin shirt. "Don't ever run away from me again," he pleaded. "I must have you for my own!"

Turning her parasol to shield them from prying eyes, Adrianna pressed her body tightly against his chest and met the fire of his kisses. Around them gentle wavelets ebbed and flowed. Oblivious to the white froth swishing their ankles, they stood enthralled by the wonder of their love.

Suddenly they realized that the earth was moving beneath their feet. Allured by the tide, sand was swirling out from under them. Laughing, they hopped through egg-white waves toward higher ground.

"Mr. Ed-wards," called a croaking voice.

They turned, blushing, to see Ben standing above them on a sand dune they had thought protected them from view.

The boy cupped his hands to his mouth and called louder. "They're a'wantin' you to crank one a'the ice-cream churns."

"Ice cream!" Adrianna exclaimed. "Way out here? Where will the ice come from?"

Laughing, Fry looked at her and licked his lips as if to say she was more delicious than ice cream. "Didn't you see those big blocks loaded at the Apalachicola wharf? The ice came from a ship just in from New England." Foy took her elbow and they reluctantly followed Ben.

The ice cream was made with great ceremony. Curiously, Adrianna watched Foy's family.

"When I live with Senator Atherton and Ma-ma, we mostly eat in restaurants," she said. "I've never had the fun of making ice cream before."

Her appetite whetted when Emma poured a thick, creamy custard into various ice-cream freezers.

"It's a cooked custard made rich with eggs," Emma explained.

"We'll leave some plain vanilla. When it's nearly frozen, we'll add wild strawberries to one, mulberries to another." Emma smiled warmly at Adrianna, as if trying hard to make her feel included. "This is our family's favorite, sherbet made from strong, sweet lemonade. Lemons grow here in great abundance."

Jonathan took the filled churns from her, placed them in wooden buckets, and attached cranks.

Beau and Win were playing with a miniature churn. Adrianna watched in surprise as Lily filled it with custard.

"I thought it was a toy."

"Oh, no," replied Lily. "It really freezes cream. Making cream is one of the *simple* pleasures *our* family enjoys."

Adrianna made no reply. She felt chilled by the wariness in Lily's eyes and the slight edge to her voice. Not knowing how to help, she sat down on a crate to watch.

Foy's muscles bulged as he rotated one of the cranks. He turned and smiled up at her. She shivered delightedly. She knew that Foy was the only man she would ever love. Green Bethune had flattered her, but she had not loved him as she did Foy. She sighed as the spring breeze kissed her cheek.

"We'd better not let you stick yo' finger in the ice cream," Jonathan said, laughing. "It would make it too sweet."

She focused her eyes to see Jonathan adding layers of ice and salt around Foy's spinning churn. He grinned at Adrianna and winked. "Takes brains instead of muscle to add the salt. Too much salt causes a skim to freeze too quickly at the edge."

Feeding Foy a piece of ice while he puffed and changed arms on the crank, Adrianna sighed with pleasure. As other men offered to turn the freezers, she noticed a mischievous gleam dancing in Foy's eye.

"Yeeeek!" she screamed. "You rascal!" Shivering as a cold globule slid down her spine, she clapped at the ice he had slipped down her back. Playfully, she chased him, whacking him with her parasol.

When the churns began to stall, they were opened. After the salty ice was carefully brushed away, the paddles were removed and Jonathan packed ice and paper over each churn to keep it frozen until after lunch. Everyone vied for the paddles. Heads close together, Foy and Adrianna licked the fluffy ice cream from the blades. Next they sampled the lemon sherbet.

"Be careful," warned Foy as he wiped the tangy juice running down her chin. "The sherbet will freeze the roof of your mouth and knock the top of your head off." He bent closer and whispered, "Like you do me."

Adrianna smiled wistfully at Foy and longed to touch his face, so fun-loving, yet serious. She knew that she enticed him, but her tumultuous feelings had gone far beyond mere attraction.

"I'll bet you say that to every girl you take on an excursion," she said, flinging out the words coquettishly. She tried to be saucy and bright, but the fear that he romanced other girls stabbed sharply. When the party was over, she must go—but where? After being with Foy every day, she could not bear the thought of leaving him.

"Adrianna," Foy whispered so close behind that his breath tickled her ear. "You don't know how special you are. My life hasn't had time for love." He inhaled against her fragrant hair. "I meant it when I said I'd been waiting for you. But your life has been so full."

"No," she whispered. "It's been empty without you."

Inches away, his arms hovered. Tingling from Foy's nearness, she ached to feel the security of his embrace, to pour out the hurts of her lonely childhood. She must assure Foy of her need, her lasting love.

Foy's tanned face paled beneath his sun-streaked hair. "I still don't have much to offer, but—Dare I hope . . ." Obviously shaken by the emotions playing over her delicate face, he took her elbow. "Come. Let's get away from the crowd."

"Lunch time!" Lily's voice called them back. "Adrianna dear." Lily smilingly summoned. "Come tell Minnie Bray and Mattie Walker about your new painting techniques. All we know how to do is sketch and make watercolor daisies."

After lunch, Adrianna excused herself to return to the steamer and don her new American bathing suit, a dress of light blue flannel with bands of navy braid around the square neck and short puffed sleeves. The skirt was daringly cropped to her knees. The scalloped hem revealed tight, matching bloomers caught with a frill of scallops just below her knees. Black cotton stockings clung to the calves of her long, slim legs.

Stepping into rubber slippers, Adrianna hurried back across the beach toward Mignonne. Struggling through the deep sand in ankle-laced, high-heeled shoes, the girl also wore a blue, braid-trimmed flannel dress. Adrianna's eyes widened as she noticed that Mignonne's bustle-style skirt fell well below her knees, and below that long, bloused bloomers covered her calves.

Apprehensively, Adrianna jerked around so quickly that her blue bandanna slipped off and her flaming hair tumbled from its pins. The older ladies were wrapped in voluminous, ground-sweeping capes. Lily was concealed by a peplumed jacket over full length trousers. With her cheeks burning, Adrianna swallowed hard. Islay and Minnie had bared their forearms, but Adrianna's calves in their clinging black cotton stockings were the only visible limbs.

Adrianna blinked at the glare-dazzled scene. As she drew back, she had an impression of shocked faces, cold with condemnation. Suddenly, she focused on the fire snapping from Lily's eyes.

nine

Adrianna remained the focal point in the silent scene of shocked disapproval. Panic-stricken, she suddenly heard an artificial chuckle penetrating the silence. Foy! She had hoped to escape before he saw her. Frantically she clapped her hand to her tumbling hair. Scooping up her fallen bandanna, she prepared to flee.

"Come on in; the water's fine," Foy said with false heartiness.

"I—maybe I shouldn't get too much sun," Adrianna stammered. She pulled her elbow away from his grasp.

Foy's voice dropped to an intimate whisper. "I love to count new freckles. Come on."

Running lightly into the warm Gulf waters, they splashed through foaming waves until they stood waist deep. Through the crystal water, Adrianna's black-stockinged calves were clearly visible. Looking like a little boy in his striped, short-sleeved suit, he grinned at her mischievously. She let out a relieved breath that she was screened from the view of those on shore.

Spanning her waist with strong hands, Foy lifted her gently as they jumped to ride the gentle swells. Adrianna wished *she* could stay in Foy's embrace and never have to walk back up on that beach.

Squeals of laughter came from Mignonne and her group of friends playing nearby, yet Adrianna and Foy felt joyfully alone. When a sudden breaker foamed over her head, Adrianna coughed and spluttered, tasting salt.

Gleefully, Foy pulled her out to deeper water, higher waves. As the roaring surf arched over them, he pulled her close. Cradled in the curve of the wave, they clung, kissing as the white cap cascaded over.

Breathlessly exhilarated, they rose and fell with the gentle surf. Adrianna's bandanna was snatched away by the changing tide. Her long hair floated about her laughing face. Her muscles were tiring, but Adrianna hated to see summoning arms motioning them back to shore.

They paddled back to shallow water. On her stomach, Adrianna walked her hands on the white-sand bottom and let her legs float behind in the foam at the tips of the waves. How could she stand up? The wet stockings stuck to her long legs. She lay limply, dreading the staring eyes of all those she must walk past to reach the steamer. The tide pushed her upward, scraping her stomach on the sand.

Childish shrieks drew haughty faces around. Beau and Win shouted with delight as the incoming tide filled their moat. They screeched with horror as the relentless waves washed away their sand castle.

Adrianna wished she could wash away clear to China. Snatching the moment of distraction, she stood. Her shaking legs were too weak to run. An arm closed around her shoulders and wrapped her in the concealing folds of a ground-sweeping cape. Surprised, she looked down into Mignonne's eyes.

"I'll never forget this," Adrianna whispered. Thankful tears trickled through the salt on her cheeks. Pulling the dark blue hood over her flaming hair, she clutched the flapping cape around her quivering legs. "I'll love you forever!"

Smiling in silent satisfaction, Mignonne walked across

the island with Adrianna and up the gangplank. The girls turned to look back, sorry to end the enchanting day.

Adrianna had hoped St. George's Island would be remembered as the place Foy pledged undying love, but she had made another silly blunder. Sadly, she knew herself to be her own worst enemy.

As the tide swallowed the island, the romance of the day washed away. Foy had disappeared in the bustle of departure. Yawning drowsily, Adrianna thanked Mignonne again and bid her good-night. As she turned toward her stateroom, she lifted drooping eyelids to see Foy gazing down at her with a look that said he, too, hoped for a good-night kiss.

"I thought all day we'd get to talk alone," he breathed against her face. He guided her toward a shadowed spot across the moon-washed deck. "I wanted to ask you—but every time . . ."

"Scientists say the moon . . ." Jonathan's jovial voice broke in upon them. "The moon's going down much quicker nowadays."

Surprised, Adrianna looked over Foy's shoulder at the white satin moon which seemed near enough to touch.

"I'm sure you'll agree, Foy," Jonathan continued into their silence. "It's going down lots faster now than when you were a lad waiting for darkness so you could hide and shoot your chinaberry popgun."

They all laughed. Catching Emma's meaningful look, Adrianna bid them good night. *Were the chaperones merely clearing the decks of dream-struck young people, she wondered. Or are they scandalized and trying to keep Foy away from me?*

Drowsy from sun and sea and sand, Adrianna immediately fell into heavy sleep, but when she awoke next morning, she lay brooding. She dreaded to go on deck. She imagined all the things people must be saying behind her back. There was no other way to see Foy, and at last, dressing gingerly because of her sunburn, she ventured out. Foy did not appear. She sat miserably fanning her hot face imagining reasons why. Adrianna finally sought out Mignonne. With evident pleasure that her friendship had been accepted, the girl readily left her group. She came quickly back with the news that Mr. Trimmer, complaining bitterly that fish and ice cream had made him sick, had retired to his quarters. Foy was standing double watches.

Not daring to go uninvited to the pilothouse and give tongues more reason to wag, Adrianna had started back to her cabin when Jonathan Ramsey called to her from his deck chair.

"Come join me," he said, patting the chair beside him.

Normally, Jonathan's twinkling eyes and lively expression made his lined face comfortably pleasant, but his eyes probed too deeply and his voice dropped a shade too intimately as he said, "I'd like to talk with you." Unable to think of an excuse, Adrianna sank glumly into a chair beside Foy's uncle. Her eyes became icy gray as she withdrew inside herself, shutting away the expected scolding.

Jonathan settled an open book on his knees. "Adrianna," his voice softened with words meant only for her ears. "Meeting you has changed my life."

Adrianna stiffened warily. If her skimpy attire had made him misconstrue her character, she certainly had never suspected this side of him.

"You're a brilliant as well as beautiful woman," Jonathan continued slowly. "Emma turned my life around. She helped me through the bad times of losing everything I thought mattered; my child, my home—even my foot, which I can get along just as well without." He laughed shortly. "But something was still missing."

Gazing deeply at the discomfited girl, he laid his big hand restrainingly on her arm and continued earnestly. "Until I met you I thought I'd given my life to Christ's Lordship. I've been making lay talks, trying to help myself and others overcome the bitterness of losing our homes and our fortunes to the War of the Sixties, but . . ."

Dismayed, Adrianna drew back. She exhaled thankfully as she noticed Emma approaching from the far end of the deck.

"You're intelligent," Jonathan repeated. "Pursuing varied interests is fine to a point, but—" He cleared his throat. "Since the war, so many new theories and religions have arisen that I don't wonder you're confused. You need the certainty of truth."

Embarrassed, Adrianna jerked her chin defiantly. "What is truth?"

Jonathan smiled tenderly. "Jesus said, 'I am the way, the truth, and the life.'" Jonathan flipped the pages of his book—she saw it was the Bible—from John 14 to First Corinthians 3. He held it for her to see as he read the eleventh verse.

"'For other foundation can no man lay than that is laid, which is Jesus Christ. Now if any man build upon this foundation gold, silver, precious stones . . .'"

Adrianna bristled, wondering if he was saying she built her life on materialism.

"'Wood, hay, stubble,'" he continued. "'Every man's work shall be made manifest . . . it shall be revealed by fire.'"

Jonathan beamed at her as if she should understand, but Adrianna felt thoroughly confused. Relief flooded her as Emma joined them. Placid Emma always seemed to make pleasant any situation.

Rising to greet her and take flight, Adrianna was again restrained by Jonathan's hand on her arm.

"I was telling Adrianna," he smiled up at his wife, "that watching her struggle to find direction has changed my life. I've told God to take my life and do with it what He will."

Emma waited in quiet expectancy.

"I believe God is calling me to preach," Jonathan said firmly. He smiled enthusiastically at Adrianna and then looked into Emma's face. "I believe God wants me to help lead this confused generation back to the Bible. They must be told that the teachings of men may seem right, but they will prove to be very wrong. God's Word will stand forever as a foundation for life and a guide to joyful living. What would you think about being a preacher's wife?"

"I think that would be wonderful!"

As Emma's silver-blonde head came down in an unaccustomed public display of affection, Jonathan raised his face to receive her kiss.

Slipping away from the pair, Adrianna went to her stateroom.

The *Mignonne Wingate* sped all too swiftly upstream, ending the excursion. Adrianna remained closeted in her stateroom nursing both her sunburn and her feeling that everyone was talking about her.

I must be a terrible person, she thought morosely.

When she did join the group, everyone seemed sunburned, drowsy, and subdued. Moments alone with Foy were few because Mr. Trimmer remained off duty and Foy feared leaving his steamboat too long in the hands of the young striker.

They shared a few snatched kisses in secluded corners, but a lump remained in Adrianna's throat. Did Foy merely enjoy kissing her and having a good time? Or had he drawn away because his family did not approve?

She was sitting on deck beside Islay Reeves one afternoon when Islay broke their companionable silence.

"What are your next plans?" she asked. "It must be fun to move about the world. Are you going back to Washington?"

"Ummm," Adrianna responded. She sighed. *What indeed*, she wondered. She had no excuse to stay in Eufaula. She must telegraph Isadora. She lifted troubled eyes to her new friend. "What did you say?"

"I said," repeated Islay, "that you must stay until after the drills and the ball."

"Drills?" Adrianna repeated distractedly.

"Fire drills." Islay nodded enthusiastically. "Every spring, fire companies from Alabama and Georgia gather for the annual convention. Eufaula has an ongoing rivalry for the silver cup with Americus, Georgia. Next week's picnic and ball will be the highlight of our social season. You simply must stay!"

"Of course she must!" Foy's deep voice made them jump. He had appeared from nowhere. His cheeks seemed slack with relief when Adrianna gravely agreed to stay.

He settled down beside her with a grinning report that Trimmer had insisted upon taking the boat through Moccasin Slough. Suddenly Adrianna felt alive again. She had one week's reprieve.

All too soon they were back in Eufaula.

Islay had invited her to spend the week as her houseguest, and Lily had insisted that she stay with the Wingates. Fearful of time alone with Lily, Adrianna declared that the Central Hotel accommodations were fine and that the host's wife, Mrs. Billings, took personal care of her. She would stay there until she contacted her grandparents.

Even though Foy looked tired and unkempt from his double watches, he insisted upon escorting her as she checked into the Central Hotel. Deep in her own thoughts, Adrianna scarcely noticed where she was going as Foy guided her across the hotel lobby.

"Ooof!" she coughed as his elbow rammed her sharply in the ribs.

"Good grannies! What's *he* doing here?" Foy growled.

Befuddled, Adrianna followed Foy's glare. Green! How could she ever contend with these two at once?

Muttering under his breath, Foy pulled her behind a potted palm. Too late. Green came striding across the room and clapped him on the shoulder of his rumpled suit.

"Foy, old boy," Green said with insufferable politeness. "So sorry I missed that grand excursion on yo' little steamer." Then with a sweeping bow, he kissed Adrianna's trembling hand. "Miss Adrianna, you are posi-tive-ly glowing like a golden goddess."

"A bit too much sun." Adrianna giggled nervously. "Whatever are you doing here, Mr. Bethune?" She withdrew her hand and reached for her ivory fan. Retreating behind it, she fanned rapidly.

"Why, I'm here for the Volunteer Firemen's Convention. What better time to sell fire insurance?" Green beamed at her. "I lie." Green dropped his blond, curly head in mock abjection. "My business is merely an excuse. New York became boring without you. I could not wait for you to return."

From the corner of her eye, Adrianna saw Foy's jaw muscle

twitching. She spoke coquettishly to turn aside the force of Green's words. "Sir! You do go on—charming every lady in sight."

"No, really," Green said sincerely. "I hear there's to be a picnic after the competitions. You must do me the honor of accompanying me—"

"She's agreed to go to the ball with me," Foy interrupted gruffly.

"I . . . um," Adrianna stuttered. Foy was merely assuming. She looked from one to the other. "Gentlemen." She sighed with genuine weariness. "You simply must let me check into my room and get some rest." When they both voiced protestations, she said firmly, "Mr. Bethune, I shall be delighted to attend the picnic with you. And Mr. Edwards." She turned upon him her most dazzling smile. "I'll go with you to the ball."

Crashing cymbals and stridently tooting cornets drew Adrianna to the window of her hotel room. Looking down into the street, she saw a brass band rounding the corner and knew the parade was about to begin.

The climax of the fun-filled week was upon her. Sighing, she placed a small pink hat squarely on her head. Studying herself in the mirror, she reflected that she had not tried to use Green to make Foy jealous, but Green seemed to have nothing but leisure to pay her court. She tilted the hat saucily over her right eye. Securing it with two six-inch hat pins, she remembered how Foy had seemed to be working day and night. He had looked tired and tense when he took her to the skating tournament and had said very little when they attended the Eufaula Library Society musical soirée.

Adrianna was at once glad and sorry that her visit was

concluding. She twirled before the looking glass for one last check of her appearance and picked up a parasol which she would surely need against the hot June sun. Fortifying herself with a long, deep breath, she went out to meet the day.

Adrianna threaded her way through the chattering crowd in the hotel lobby. Reaching the appointed place on Broad Street, she found Foy's family. Emma introduced her to her special friends, Mrs. Chauncey Rhodes and Mrs. William Simpson.

Adrianna looked from one to the other in confusion. They were identical twins.

"Don't worry if you can't keep them straight," said Jonathan, chuckling. "They had a double wedding and—wasn't it Mr. Simpson who tried to escort Elizabeth from the church instead of his bride, Mollie?" Laughter pulled their group into a companionable circle. Adrianna relaxed. She would not worry about Foy and Green today. She would simply enjoy the excitement.

Her attention was upon the ceremony naming the Cleburne fire company's new engine for Islay Reeves. Watching her friend Islay, Adrianna did not see Foy as he approached. His hand brushed the shining hair spilling down her back, and she turned a sparkling smile upon him. Foy inhaled and rolled his eyes heavenward.

Engulfed in whistles and cheers as Mayor Wells J. Bray led the parade before them, Adrianna gave half attention to the first group bearing the banner, "E.B. Young Fire Company," and pulling a handsome engine and hose reel. As they marched smartly in their dark blue coats and black pantaloons, she thought about the two men in her life. Green noticed and complimented everything she wore while Foy scarcely said a word. *But, oh, his reactions*, she thought and backed a fraction closer to him as cheers rose again.

"Peep through here," Foy said, pointing. "I don't want you to miss the 'Oceanics' from Brunswick, Georgia. They claim to give the impression of the Atlantic Ocean with their uniforms, and—" Adrianna caught a glimpse of the blue caps, white shirts, blue pants, and red stockings just as the banner, "City by the Sea," began to shake.

Next came the Phoenix Company, marching with a whirling display of Japanese parasols; the Chattahoochee Number Five; another brass band; and companies visiting from across Alabama and Georgia. Last of all came Eufaula's hook and ladder company.

"Most towns have engine companies and hose companies," said Foy. "But only a few have a rig like this," he added proudly.

His voice was drowned out by cheering as the parade ended with the carriage of the Eufaula fire department chief, Dan Rowlett. Riding triumphantly around him were six tiny girls waving the colors. Laughing, Adrianna joined in the clapping.

Foy squeezed an arm around her in the press of the crowd moving toward the Firemanic tournament.

The Mechanics of Americus came first in the reel contest. The reel was stationed one hundred yards from the engine. The men stood at attention. A sand bag dropped on signal. The squad ran, carrying the reel to the engine, and began attaching hose.

"They look so serious," commented Adrianna.

"It's an important drill, a matter of honor, and two hundred dollars in gold are at stake," Foy explained. "But their time is too slow, and see, they didn't play their water all the way to that flagman."

Adrianna was tiring by the next set of contests, but Foy urged her to watch a little longer.

"You must see the Phoenix Company," Foy said laughing. "We call them the 'Toe-nails.'"

"Why?" She cut her eyes flirtatiously from under her pink hat.

"Just wait," he said teasingly.

She watched the company fill their tank at the cistern. The men took their positions, then removed their shoes and socks. The chief shouted through a silver megaphone as the men dug their feet into the ground and attacked the hand pump madly.

"The 'Toe-nails' say they pump better because they get a good purchase on the ground with their toes," Foy laughed. "Listen to the German jeweler, Schrieber."

Adrianna followed his pointing finger to the little man who held the hose nozzle. Straining forward, she caught his agonized shout.

"Vater, vater, gif me vater!"

She turned her face into Foy's shoulder to hide her giggles.

"It's a local by-word among us boys." Foy chuckled. "But I'm sure bud thirsty. Let's duck into Besson's Drug Store for a strawberry soda."

"You have sodas *here*?" Adrianna clapped her hands.

"Sure we do," he said, looking hurt at her surprise. "We've had a mineral water factory for ages, and soda water—" He shrugged. "Maybe five years."

Adrianna grimaced, sorry that Foy had caught her implication. In New York City, Green had frequently taken her to soda fountains, but she had not expected to find the treat this far from—the word which popped into her brain was civilization. She was thankful she had not spoken it aloud.

Why did I have to think about Green? Adrianna moaned inwardly as she looked up and saw the handsome man had followed them into the drug store.

Green pulled up another wrought iron chair and joined them at the small, glass table without being asked. "Good morning, good morning," Green said heartily. "You have sodas," he said, raising his eyebrows, "*here*?"

Foy glowered but said nothing.

"I didn't expect the custom to have spread this soon." After all of his exclaiming over their sodas, Green ordered a ginger ale.

"It isn't—is it t . . . time for the p . . . picnic?" Adrianna stammered. She had thought she had overcome her stuttering, but the animosity between the two men shook her.

"There are lots more contests before the picnic." Green beamed at her. "Right now, I'm doing a little wagering. How 'bout it, Edwards?" Green turned to Foy. Whipping out a leather wallet, he extracted a thousand dollar bill and waved it tantalizingly. "This says Eufaula's E.B. Youngs will lower the record of the Wide-Awakes from Americus."

Adrianna gasped. She had not known such a large bill was printed. Understanding Foy had no money to spare foolishly, she touched his arm restrainingly. He grinned crookedly at her and shook his head.

Green raised his voice loud enough for everyone in the drug store to hear. "I understand those two teams are the big rivals—but is this too rich for your blood?"

Foy snorted disgustedly. "I work too hard for my money to—"

"I know you don't carry cash around," Green interrupted. "An IOU will do fine. Miss Adrianna will hold the bets."

"No!" Foy spoke with calm firmness. "I'm not a gambling man," he said pleasantly. "It's against my principles." Turning indifferently away, Foy finished his soda. "Come on. We're missing the fun."

They went out into the rapidly heating day to watch the next contests.

Cheers arose when the famous Alabama company, the E.B. Youngs, appeared on the tracks. They stood at attention as the sand bag dropped. Then they ran down the track shouting, "Hurrah!"

Adrianna watched in amazement as the runners dug quickly to the wooden water main made of hollowed logs squared and beveled to fit together. A hole had already been drilled in the pipe and plugged with a small slick of wood. The designated plugman snatched out the wooden fireplug.

A man with a stop watch yelled, "Run to the plug: 12:15."

Standing uncomfortably between Green and Foy, she waited as the pipeman made the connection with the hard rubber hose and water began to draw. As the men pumped frantically, she watched Foy's jaw muscle twitch and realized Green had not only tried to push him into betting because of her, but betting against his friends.

"Water to the flag," shouted the timekeeper. "Twenty-four!"

Next came the Pulaski Number One. They made a pretty run to the plug, but the pipeman fell down as he reached the engine. They failed to make connections and the shout went up, "A burst."

The Wide-Awakes from Americus came forward amid great cheering.

The timekeeper shouted, "Run to the plug: 12:20!"

Fanning tiredly, Adrianna felt hot and slightly sick as her two suitors watched the frantically working firemen.

"Water to the flag . . ." came the shout. "Twenty-six!"

Eufaula had won. Whistles, shouts, and stamping feet

created pandemonium. Green went smilingly off to collect his bets. Foy would have lost if Green had forced him into betting. As the Youngs received the coveted silver cup, Adrianna hid behind her fan and wiped perspiration.

Listlessly, she followed Green to the picnic. Although he was at his charming best, she did not know what he said or what she ate.

The moon rose full and clear for the great complimentary ball given by the Cleburne Fire Company on Saturday night. Moving the kerosene lamp closer to the chevel glass, Adrianna frowned at her reflection. Green would know her gown was the latest Paris style, but would it be too different from the other ladies? She had chosen pure white satin which shone with the luster of fine pearls. Trimmed only with narrow net ruching on the scooped neckline and sleeveless armholes, the dress emphasized her innocent beauty. Craning to see the back, she knew it would capture all eyes because the satin was softly crushed into cascading poufs from the bustle to the train. She pinned a pink rose in her hair as her only adornment, pulled on elbow-length white kid gloves, and went down to meet Foy.

Adrianna searched Foy's serious eyes in vain for a sign that he thought she looked like a bride. She had never known him to be so tensely silent. Had she somehow disappointed him again? An odd expression made him look like a lost little boy dressed in white tie and tails.

As the orchestra tuned up and began Mr. Strauss's latest waltz, Foy wordlessly held out his white-gloved hands. Moving into his arms, Adrianna clung wistfully to his shoulder as he whirled her to the music with his long black tailcoat flapping and her white train swishing. Swaying close enough to feel the beating of each other's hearts, they spoke no words. Frightened that something between them seemed lost, Adrianna struggled to pull her charm into place when Foy's friends claimed her for occasional dances.

Suddenly Green appeared and asked her for a dance just as a polka began. Tripping over her train on the lively, jerky steps, she apologized for weariness.

"Of course you're tired," Green replied solicitously. "Let's go into the garden to cool."

Adrianna agreed without thinking.

The warm June night, heavy with the fragrance of roses, closed around them as Green led her to a secluded bench.

"You have never been more lovely, my dear," he said sincerely. Daringly, he kissed her bare neck. "You might have stepped from a painting by Renoir."

Pleased in spite of herself, she smiled softly. Green was, indeed, a highly cultured gentleman.

"I don't believe you understood . . ." He took both of her hands in his and squeezed them until she looked at him with attention. "What I was trying to tell you at the picnic is that my own plantation near Charleston is prospering again. But more than that—" He dropped a kiss on her nose and lifted her chin, urging her to look at him. "My fleet of ships will again be carrying cotton to Liverpool. How would you like to see London and Paris?" His voice rose excitedly. "I want to show you the world!"

Adrianna drew back, mouth agape.

"Beautiful creature!" Green dropped to one knee beside her. "Will you do me the honor of becoming my wife?"

Shocked, Adrianna looked at Green kneeling humbly before her. Then her eyes narrowed and hardened to a cold gray. She knew that the time had come for her to grow up. Jonathan had told her to set a course for her life and stick to it.

"Green, I—" Her voice squeaked. "I'm flattered. You're such a cultured gentleman. Seeing the world with you . . ." Trembling, she knew she would fit far better into Green's realm than in this small town with these overly religious people. "I'm all aflutter." She pressed her hands against her chest, turning back the acceptance which formed on her lips. "Please . . ." She tried to appear demure. "May I have until tomorrow to answer? Tomorrow night?"

Green kissed her palms. "Only 'til Sunday night, my lovely. I'm leaving for New York on the Monday morning train."

"Yes," she murmured. "I must leave, too—to visit my mother." Sighing, she knew that she no longer had an excuse to stay in Eufaula. Her dreams of being a fairy princess in the castle tower of Barbour Hall were ebbing away as swiftly as the tide had destroyed the children's sand castle. The ball was almost over. Foy would be claiming her for one last dance, then taking her home. *Telling me goodbye?* Twisting her feet in their white suede dancing shoes, she thought ruefully of glass slippers and Cinderella. Yes, she must hurry and leave Eufaula because her carriage was turning into a pumpkin.

ten

Foy pummeled his pillow. This should have been one of the happiest nights of his life. He had planned to propose to Adrianna after the ball. She had looked so beautiful, so like a bride, and he had not even told her. He had endured the dance, repeatedly rehearsing his speech. The hour was upon him when Adrianna returned from the garden with Green. She had seemed remote, unattainable.

Green! Savagely, Foy flung the pillow across the bedroom. *It's all Green's fault*!

No. He dropped his head in his hands. *Green was not on the boat. But Lily was and . . .*

He had thought he was communicating his love and his desire to make her his bride. Every time they had been alone and he had primed himself to extract a promise from her, they had been interrupted. He suspected Lily had planned some of the diversions.

Oh, Lily had been broad-minded enough about the bathing suit, but Adrianna's flippant attitude about the Bible had made Lily argue long and hard that he should try to bring Adrianna to Christ before they married. Her impassioned words rattled in his brain.

"Foy, you know that Paul says we should not marry just to be marrying, but to marry 'only in the Lord,' " Lily had insisted. "Remember that Second Corinthians 6:14 says, 'Be ye not unequally yoked together with unbelievers: for what fellowship hath righteousness with unrighteousness?' "

"But Adrianna is a sweet, good person," Foy had replied.

"Darling Foy, you know being a Christian does not mean being a good person. It means acknowledging that we have sinned by missing the mark of the high calling of God. We can never be righteous enough on our own to bridge the separation from Him. Only as we accept Jesus' death on the cross as payment for our sins and believe in His resurrection as the evidence that we have eternal fellowship with God, do we become children of God."

Lily had reminded him of people they knew whose lasting marriages were based on the love of God. She pointed out some unhappy acquaintances whose shallow faith played no part in governing family relationships. She had cautioned him on the futility of planning to change a partner after marriage.

Acknowledging Lily's godly wisdom, Foy had agreed to take time pursuing his courtship. But Green had intervened.

Foy paced his bedroom. Perhaps Adrianna did fit better into Green's world. Miserable, Foy trudged to the thick blackness of the attic, wrestling with his problems as he climbed the familiar stairs. Emerging in the glassed belvedere, Foy saw the rosy streaks of dawn lighting the sky. His spirits lifted. Suddenly he thought what he could offer Adrianna: love, a permanent home, tenderness, and caring. *I can offer more than Green*, he thought. *I love her very soul*!

Adrianna had agreed to a brief visit on Sunday afternoon. Foy's hand shook as he opened the double doors and ushered her into Barbour Hall. He knew that his time had run out.

"What was it you wanted to show me?" Adrianna asked coolly. Fear, anger, pride, jealousy tumbled like a kaleidoscope in Foy's brain. Love and desire filled his throat, stopping words. He ground his teeth resolutely. A navy man could not give up without a try. Silently he bowed his head over

Adrianna's delicate hand and kissed her fingertips. Then he pulled her up the curving staircase to the second floor.

"This way," Foy indicated, leading her upward again through the dark passage of the attic. They remained silent until they stepped through the opening into the belvedere.

Adrianna's expression lifted with delight as she emerged in the sun-filled room. Foy watched in relief as she was drawn out of her silence.

"What a wonderful view! It's like owning the world!" Adrianna exclaimed as she turned from one windowed wall to the other and looked out across the tops of trees along the winding river.

"This has always been my special place," Foy said with small-boy eagerness. "Mine and Lily's." Seeing her smile slide, he hurried on. "I'd hoped it might be special to you. When I was a lad and Lily and Harrison were in love and struggling against the world to get married, I dreamed that one day I would be a pilot on the Chattahoochee, and, and . . ." His deep voice choked with emotion. "And my wife would be here watching for me."

Foy's voice dropped so low he wondered if she had heard. She had turned a rigid back to him. Sunlight set her hair ablaze.

Overcome, Foy crossed the small room in a step and buried his face in her hair. Hopefully, he wrapped long arms around her and held her close.

"Why would she have to stay here?" Adrianna asked in a strained voice. "Why couldn't she go with you?"

"Well." Foy laughed shakily. "I'd always imagined her at home with the house full of children, but . . ." Hopelessly, he slackened his grip. He could not bear to ask for her only to be told she was marrying Green. Releasing her, he stepped back.

Adrianna turned. Wistfully, like a love-starved child, she

looked at him, saying nothing. Foy crushed her in an embrace and kissed her trembling lips. Letting his love flow, urging her to love him, he suddenly realized Adrianna was responding joyfully.

Encouraged, he drew back and took her dimpled chin in his shaking hand to lock her gaze with his. "Adrianna, I'm crazy with love for you. I'd hoped if I waited I'd have more to offer. I can never give you what Green can, but I love you. Dare I hope you'll be my bride? Will you marry me? Now?"

For answer, Adrianna's arms went up. Twining her fingers in his hair, she spoke with her smile singing in her words. "Yes, oh, yes, Foy!' Then her voice trembled tearfully. "I . . . I've never known real affection, only approval when I did right. My wildest dreams weren't as wonderful as you loving me."

"Do you want time to think about it?" Foy asked. "Can you be happy in Eufaula? In Barbour Hall?"

"I don't need to think—unless you're not sure," she said teasingly. Then she spoke seriously. "I've never had a real home in one place." Shyly, she raised her face for his kiss. "Home, my home is here in your arms."

"And here you'll stay." Foy swept Adrianna to a special corner. With one arm securely around her, he added to the other inscriptions preserved on the wall, "Adrianna and Foy, June 5, 1876."

Then his face clouded doubtfully. "As for the house, you'll have your work cut out for you. Not one thing has been moved since Mama died. Come on. I'll take you for an inspection tour of your dilapidated mansion. I asked Kitty and Lige to be here to protect your—"

"My reputation?" Adrianna's laughter pealed. "You mean I still have one after the episode of the exposed limbs?"

Foy feigned a wicked leer. "You were delicious. But Lily, at least, took it in stride."

Adrianna looked at him with near disbelief. Then she followed him to the upstairs sitting room. Long-boned Kitty, with a self-conscious look, was puttering about the small morning room.

"Kitty," Foy said excitedly to the woman who had been his childhood nurse, "meet Miss Adrianna. She has agreed to marry me and become the new mistress of Barbour Hall."

"I'm so glad to know you," Adrianna said. "And to have you to help me with this huge house." She whispered conspiratorially, "You'll have to teach me all the things Foy likes and doesn't like."

A pleased expression spread over Kitty's face. "I been taking care of him since he wuz this high." She extended her hand. "This house been needing a lady like you."

Kitty opened the door into the adjoining blue and white bedroom which Lily and Emma had shared. She let Adrianna peep into the huge master bedroom at the rear, but she kept the door to Foy's room firmly shut. As the women conversed about the running of the house, Foy stood back in dazed happiness.

Hand in hand, the happy couple walked though the main floor. Foy suddenly realized how badly everything needed painting.

"What I'd like here is some new murals," Adrianna suggested as they stood in the spacious central hall.

"Anything your heart desires," Foy said, lifting her hand to kiss it.

"And, the curtains . . ." She stepped into the parlor. "These are really old and out of style." Frowning, she ran her fingers over the carved mahogany leaves and scrolls on the stiff-backed, double settee. "In fact there are several things in here

I'd like to change."

"Sure bud." He shrugged.

They strolled through the wildly overgrown garden where Adrianna met Lige. She charmed him with her smile.

In the white-latticed gazebo, Foy and Adrianna sat nestled silently, savoring the joy of shared love. At last Adrianna spoke. "I suppose I must leave tomorrow as I had planned,"

Shocked, Foy straightened. "I don't ever want to be parted from you again!"

Laughing lightly, she kissed his ear and said, "But I must go home to tell Mama. A bride has so many things to do!"

"But, but," Foy spluttered. He had not thought of wedding preparations. "Well, you can't leave before June eleventh," he said triumphantly. "Mignonne will be sixteen, and she'd never forgive you if you missed her coming out party!"

Reluctantly they left their haven and went to the Wingate house to share their news. Lily hugged Adrianna with welcoming arms and apologized for not being able to give an immediate engagement party.

"Oh, I couldn't take away from Mignonne's big day," Adrianna said, smiling at her young friend.

"I have the perfect solution," Harrison interposed. "There's to be a grand celebration for our nation's hundredth birthday. Senator Atherton has promised to be the July Fourth speaker. Perhaps your parents could come, too, and we'd have—"

"The wedding in July?" Foy leaned forward.

"No, no!" Lily laughed and patted him fondly. "The engagement party. You must do things properly if you expect local society to accept your bride."

When Lily invited them to stay for supper, Foy saw Adrianna's cheeks become pale. She twisted her hands and declared that she must return to the hotel.

"What's the matter?" he demanded when they were alone in the buggy.

"I promised Green that—He's waiting to—I'm to have supper with . . ."

"What?" Foy exploded. "If you're engaged to me you can't be meeting him!" Tears filled Adrianna's eyes and he relented. "I'm sorry." He patted her hand. "You didn't know we'd be engaged. But it won't hurt him to wait and wonder." Her chin trembled and he cupped it tenderly. "Send him a note."

"No. Foy, Green's going back to New York tomorrow. It's only right that I meet him and tell him about us."

"I'll go with you."

Adrianna shook her head. "Green's a proud man. I must see him alone and—tell him goodbye."

For the next few days, Foy found every possible excuse to look in at Barbour Hall. Laughing and chattering, Adrianna and Kitty were cleaning every nook and cranny.

With careful thoughts of her reputation, Adrianna had belatedly accepted Islay's invitation and moved in as her houseguest for the remainder of her stay. Foy and Adrianna had shared the news of their forthcoming marriage with close friends, and Islay, Emma, Mignonne, and Lily came over daily to help get the house prepared for another bride.

One morning Foy found Lily stamping about the parlor. With her eyes flashing, she snapped, "Mama's mahogany double settee! It was Chippendale!" Her voice rose in a wail. "A finely carved design made in 1820. Adrianna said she was replacing 'that old handmade piece,'" Lily said mockingly, "with 'modern, factory-turned chairs.'"

"Adrianna didn't know," said Foy soothingly. "Don't push her, Lily," he pleaded. "Help her. Lead her gently into the fold like you've done the rest of us."

With tears streaming down her cheeks, Lily stared at him. "No, I guess she doesn't know about the things that set gentry apart. She's going to break you!" She stormed out the door.

Foy looked around uneasily. He hoped Adrianna had not heard. She entered a few moments later and kissed him delightedly.

"I've engaged the famous French mural painter, Monsieur Le Franc, to come and paint palm-filled urns on the central-hall walls," she said gleefully. "And just wait until you see what I've planned for the music room!"

Foy felt old recalling how Mignonne had looked at her ball. No longer an adorable child, Mignonne was a stunningly beautiful woman. Adrianna had delighted him by asking Mignonne to be her maid of honor.

Since his confrontation with Lily, Foy had been edgy. He was tired of the disruption Adrianna's nesting instincts had brought to his bachelor quarters. He was almost relieved that she was spending a few weeks at home with her mother.

Without Adrianna, however, Barbour Hall seemed empty in spite of the wooden barrels which began arriving. He opened one. Spilling out straw packing, he found a set of china which was far more elaborately decorated than the set already filling the dining room.

Suddenly fearing the cost of having a wife, Foy retreated from the barrels and set out with long strides for a walk. Ambling aimlessly, he ended up at the fairgrounds and race track.

"Good grannies!" Foy bumped his head with the heel of his hand when he rounded the horse barn and spotted Green Bethune.

The arrogant man saw Foy. His mouth curved up in a one-sided smile.

Foy managed a gruff greeting. "Sure bud didn't expect to see you in the sticks again."

"Couldn't resist the temptation to challenge your local horses." Green beamed with friendly charm. "Care to wager against your town favorite, Strawberry Jack?"

Foy frowned. "I wouldn't bet against Strawberry Jack. His owner brought his know-how straight from Kentucky. His coat of arms is S.S.S., Speed, Safety, and Style."

Green's blue eyes narrowed knowingly. "Let's stir the sporting blood. What will you wager," he said, "on whom the fair Adrianna will be to wife?"

Taken aback, Foy stammered, "That bet would be taking candy from a baby, sir, She'll marry me and that right soon."

"What wager?" Green taunted.

Foy laughed hollowly. "I'd stake my life." He shrugged. "Anything. The *Mignonne Wingate*."

Green chuckled and turned as if to walk away. "So certain are you?" Suddenly he whirled and put his face near Foy's. "She told me you asked her to marry you. She's coming back to make a formal announcement after the fair. But who will it be?"

Feeling reduced to the small-boy fury which had defeated him when first he met Green Bethune, Foy ground his teeth and said nothing.

Green sneered at Foy and added, "I'll see your bet on the *Mignonne Wingate* and raise you. Obviously she didn't tell you I also proposed! I'm meeting her here for her answer. That little redhead's choice just might be your Fo'th of July fireworks!"

eleven

Adrianna alighted from the train in the Eufaula depot. Eagerly, she searched for Foy's sun-streaked hair above the milling crowd.

The people converged on Senator Atherton. Adrianna stood uncertainly with her parents. They remained unnoticed as all attention focused on the distinguished statesman and his elaborately costumed wife.

Chattering, Adrianna tried to bridge the distance between her parents.

"Oh, there he is," she squealed at last. "Come meet Foy!"

"Foy," she cried ecstatically. "This is my Mama." She smiled down at the small woman. "And Sam Atherton, my Papa! He came for our engagement party, too!"

"How do you do, Mrs. Atherton." Foy bowed. "So nice that you could come for the—festivities." He turned and said, "How do you do, sir?"

Sam Atherton stepped forward and shook hands cordially. "I'm pleased to meet Adrianna's young man."

Adrianna held out her hand, longing for Foy's touch, waiting for his gaze to wrap her in love.

Foy did not look at her.

"I'm so excited they ..." Her voice trailed as she watched Foy's stern face. "That they could come for . . ." She swallowed. *What could be wrong?* "Our formal announcement," she finished in a whisper. She stared at him. "You're still—When is Lily planning the party?"

Adrianna waited.

"She couldn't send out invitations." Foy cast her a side-long glance.

The four stood like the corners of an empty room.

"Lily had to have a final word from you." Foy shoved the words into the void.

"Oh."

"I expect she wants to know the wedding date," Mrs. Atherton contributed softly.

Foy jutted out his chin. "Uh, yes, ma'am. Something like that." He gestured them toward a carriage.

Their conversation was stiff and formal as they followed the parade to the fairgrounds. Adrianna shifted uncomfortably. Foy had never been shy about meeting strangers. She did so want her parents to love him, but he seemed determined to give them a bad impression.

As they passed through the exhibits and her mother lingered at the canned goods, Adrianna hissed, "What's wrong with you?"

"Nothing's wrong with me."

"Ohh, look at these beautiful pianos." Adrianna stepped forward quickly because Mama was watching with a puzzled frown.

"We don't need a new piano."

"No. But Foy, I would like some of these Brumby rockers for the porch." She pointed to the next exhibit. "They're big enough for rocking ba—"

"Prefer the old family furniture myself."

Adrianna turned to her father, who was conversing with a Mrs. Parker about the display of her novel pets, Texas anteaters and horned frogs.

Linking her arm with his, Adrianna lifted her chin icily and left Foy to bring her mother. The crowd moved toward the speaker's platform and Senator Atherton's booming voice.

Watching Foy's rigid back, Adrianna wiped beads of perspiration from her upper lip. Grandfather was intoning every detail of America's hundred years. Patting her hands soundlessly when the closing applause finally came, she thought that surely now she could have a moment with Foy.

A man with a megaphone announced the performance of the daring equestrienne Nellie Burke, and the crowd swept them along to the white-fenced track.

Adjusting her jostled hat, Adrianna looked up to see Foy giving her a cold look. Pushing back the straw brim, she saw Green Bethune across the track.

"Oh, no!" she wailed. "I'd hoped we'd never have to see him again!"

Foy glowered. "Don't tell me you didn't expect to see Green. He said you were coming back to choose between us. That you told him to meet you here!"

"And you believed him? Oh, Foy." She turned close against him. "You know it's you I love. I told him I was marrying you."

"Miss Adrianna, your beauty increases with each passing day."

Adrianna jumped as Green's voice penetrated her misery. Somehow he had pushed his way through the crowd. Adrianna managed to introduced him to her parents.

Green put on his most charming manner. "Mr. Atherton, you must place your bets on the best horse, Charleston's Pride!" He chuckled. "Unless you want to lose your money on the local favorite—what was that little ole horse, Foy, Strawberry Jack?"

"Foy! You didn't gamble?" Adrianna asked anxiously behind her fan.

Foy's retort was drowned out by cheering for Nellie Burke's barrel racing, but when Adrianna tugged at his sleeve, he repeated, "I can depend on Strawberry Jack."

"Didn't you think you could depend on me?"

Foy ducked his head and rubbed a crimson ear. "I—wasn't sure. Grannies, woman, you're driving me crazy. If you really love me, let's get married as soon as possible." He slipped his arm around her.

"As soon as possible." She nodded solemnly.

Wild cheering rang out again as the harness racers trotted on the track. Relieved to find the source of Foy's strange behavior, yet frightened at Green's continuing interference, Adrianna folded her fan and gnawed it nervously.

Swaying in the heat, Adrianna did not feel a part of the roaring crowd. She did not understand the source of the frenzy over Strawberry Jack until she looked at Green's angry face. He was not accustomed to losing.

The Atherton party was next ushered to Hart's Hall where the old families of Eufaula were celebrating with a great Centennial Tea Party. Green did not follow, and Foy behaved more normally as he introduced her parents to his family. Jonathan offered his arm to Adrianna's mother saying, "You must have a delicacy from each food table. The ladies have outdone themselves decorating. See, there is fruit from Georgia, palmetto and rice from South Carolina, minerals from Pennsylvania, pines from North Carolina . . ."

Relieved that her mother was thus escorted, Adrianna thought to escape for a moment to make things right with Foy, but her grandmother caught her arm.

"You must carry my plate," Isadora said, critically surveying the room. "I'm glad to see the ladies have become cognizant of fashion."

Adrianna looked about her. The dresses were styled with the latest cord-pleat trimming and gophering and the tremendous hats were adorned with gold-colored silk velvet flowers, gold-spangled plumes, or fruit ornaments.

"You need not trouble yourself about my lack of society, Ma-ma," Adrianna said. "These people are of fine old families. Now, admit it, you've never seen more elegant diamonds, and the coiffures are *à la Grecque*."

"I suppose so," Isadora agreed reluctantly. "But your young man exhibits an uncouth gruffness. You must polish—"

"It's just that we've had a—a slight misunderstanding."

Adrianna's anxiety increased with each passing hour. The two family groups dined at Rowlett's Restaurant, conversing nervously.

Night fell at last, but the heat of the day did not cool. Neither did Foy's temper. As the party left the restaurant for the hotel, he silently guided Adrianna to a small runabout. They had a moment alone at last.

As the horse clopped into the darkness, Adrianna dropped the cloak of reserve she had clung to all day. "Oh, Foy, how could you think I'd—"

"Why should Green lie?"

"Because Green is Green!" Adrianna lifted her chin defiantly, then sagged. "Perhaps I should have told you. But . . ." She nestled against him. "It didn't seem worth mentioning."

Foy did not respond.

Straightening, she blurted, "Yes, he asked me to marry him. I can't help that."

Tight-lipped, Foy stared unseeingly ahead of the horse. "Green," he said, spitting out the word, "Green said you'd choose between us when you came for the Fourth."

"That's not true!"

Reaching out with trembling fingertips, Adrianna turned Foy's hurt face close to hers. "I've loved you from the moment I saw you, but I didn't know you loved me. And I allowed Green to court me, but . . ."

One finger stroked his red-tipped ear. She thought back to that Sunday night when she had given Green her answer and shivered at the recollection of the angry scene.

"Green proposed before you did. I asked him to give me time to answer. No, wait," she begged as Foy stiffened and turned away. "I had given up hope that you'd ask me. But don't you remember? When you did ask, I said yes instantly!"

Foy relaxed slightly.

"I met Green on Sunday night because I'd promised an answer. I told Green that I would marry you. That we'd announce it formally when I came for the Centennial Celebration."

"That was your mistake." Foy slapped the reins at the barely moving horse. "You shouldn't have let him know that. Never give Green an inch."

"He won't come between us anymore." Not worrying about an unladylike advance, Adrianna kissed his ear. "It's you I love and you I want to marry—if you still want me."

Saying nothing, Foy directed the buggy beneath an ancient cedar and dropped the reins. Wrapping Adrianna in a crushing embrace, he kissed her, pouring out despair and longing. His soul filled with joy as she responded.

"Tomorrow, let's set the date for the engagement party and the wedding," he urged when it seemed he could trust his voice.

"Tomorrow," she promised.

Adrianna beamed at her parents as she and Foy showed them through Barbour Hall the next morning.

"Quite impressive," said Sam Atherton as they crossed the black and white marble floor of the central hall.

Foy proudly showed Sam the pine timbers, which had been cut on the property and allowed to season three years before the house was built in 1854.

While the men were occupied, Adrianna showed her mother some of the modernizing she planned. In the back hall she pointed to the black couch with S-shaped legs and said, "I want to get rid of that horsehair sofa with those funny legs and put in a new Turkish divan."

Lily joined them in the parlor. Graciously putting the Athertons at ease, she related her plans for the engagement party. "I told Foy that to set the wedding sooner than three months after the engagement was formally announced would be improper."

Disappointed, Adrianna nodded meekly.

"October then?"

Mary Atherton nodded in agreement.

"You'd better check the Senator's schedule," Sam Atherton said sardonically.

"Where will we have the wedding?" Lily asked tentatively.

Adrianna panicked. Knowing that the bride's home was customary, she looked from one parent to the other, thought of her grandparents, and wondered, *Where is my home*? She stared at Lily and found understanding in her eyes.

Lily said, "Since your family is so . . . cosmopolitan—perhaps Eufaula? Our church is—"

"Oh, yes!" Adrianna clapped her hands delightedly. "Eufaula, since our family's so scattered. Can't you," she said, looking pleadingly from one parent to the other, "come back to Eufaula?" Receiving their nod, she ran into the hall. "But not the church.

Here. Right here. I want to come down that beautiful stairway." Her voice rose excitedly. "Can't you just picture that, Foy?"

"Perfectly."

"And the reception. Oh, it must be in this lovely dining room. Come, you haven't seen the most beautiful part of the house!"

Tugging at her parents' hands, she hurried them into the music room. "Mr. Le Franc has moved into the house for three months to hand paint the walls. It's quite elaborate, I know." She felt suddenly uncertain. "But he uses such delicate hues that—"

"It's lovely," murmured Mrs. Atherton, testing the paint of the fleur-de-lis stenciled on the walls.

Sam Atherton threw back his head to see the ceiling. It looked like a blue sky filled with clouds and butterflies. He grinned and said fondly, "It looks like you, pudding."

"Thank you, Papa. And you *will* give me away?" Tears of happiness filled her eyes as he squeezed her hand in assent. Adrianna turned their attention upward.

"Mr. Le Franc brings in the flowers from the garden to paint. See, each corner is different." She pointed to lilies, pansies, roses, and tulips.

"He's a very fine artist," replied Lily. "The hollyhock on that door panel has such depth."

Adrianna met Foy's eyes across the room and reveled in their oneness. "Look at the dining room," she babbled. "Mr. Le Franc was intrigued with the design on the silver, and he added that to this ceiling and wall. Didn't Foy tell me that y'all buried this silver in the garden when the Yankees came? And oh, Mama, can't you just see a wedding cake on this beautiful mahogany table beneath that glorious Waterford chandelier?"

The cake was magnificent indeed as it waited beneath the

chandelier for the wedding to begin. Emma had claimed the honor of making it from the recipe she had used for Lily and Harrison. Admiring the towering masterpiece, Adrianna could smell the aroma of fruit, mace, and nutmeg through the glistening white frosting.

When Adrianna and her family had returned to Eufaula for the wedding, moved up to September 17 to accommodate Senator Atherton's schedule, Barbour Hall had turned into a fairyland of roses. Foy explained that their neighbor, Mrs. Kendall, had sent bouquets of long-stemmed beauties from the thousands of bushes in her garden. Smiling, Adrianna knew this gift from the grandest mansion in town gave their marriage a stamp of approval from local society. She inhaled the sweetness and drifted up the stairs to the sunny bedroom where she was to dress.

The time had come at last. Adrianna fumbled with the tiny satin buttons from the neck to the pointed waist of the closely fitted bodice. She had chosen a simply styled wedding gown to set off her dazzling hair. The brocaded satin skirt showed the embossed roses only in a glimmer when she moved.

Mignonne helped her drape an airy lace overskirt down one side. Silently she placed the gossamer veil over Adrianna's flaming hair and blushing face.

Mignonne tiptoed out to peep down the stairs.

"It's time," she whispered as if afraid to break the spell. "Everyone is assembled in the parlor." She handed Adrianna a bouquet of white roses and dainty tuberoses and clutched her own nosegay of pink that matched her pink bridesmaid dress. "I hope you and Foy will live happily ever after." She went out to take her place.

Papa joined Adrianna in the upstairs hall. Gripping his arm, she walked down the short flight to the landing and paused.

The soft notes floating from the music room ceased.

Emma struck the stirring chords of the "Wedding March." Adrianna floated down the remaining stairs and paused for a moment beneath the chandelier's crown of thorns.

In the parlor, an altar of glossy magnolia leaves and delicate lanceleaf smilax was banked before the white marble fireplace. Jonathan waited, an open Bible in his hand. Beside him, Harrison stood stalwartly as best man. Beau and Win, in sailor suits, wore grins as wide as the collars flapping on their shoulders. They flanked either side, holding satin pillows bearing rings. Mignonne waited expectantly. Sweeping them in a brief, loving glance, Adrianna looked at Foy. Elegantly handsome in his trim, naval uniform of Confederate gray with his sword on his hip, Foy waited with his face alight with love.

Releasing a tremulous breath, Adrianna drifted toward Foy.

"Dearly beloved," said Jonathan in a warm voice. "We are gathered together here in the sight of God, and in the face of this company, to join together this man and this woman in holy matrimony." He paused to smile, and his twinkling eyes eased Adrianna's trembling. "Marriage was divinely instituted when Jehovah God spoke the nuptial words to Adam and Eve in the Garden of Eden. Jesus of Nazareth honored its celebration by his presence at the wedding in Cana of Galilee, and chose its beautiful relations as the figure of that union between himself and his Church. Into this holy estate, these two persons come now to be joined." Jonathan's voice gentled. He was asking for Foy's vow. "Wilt thou love her, comfort her, honor and keep her, in sickness and in health; and, forsaking all others, keep thee only unto her, so long as ye both shall live?"

"I will!" Foy answered strongly.

Jonathan turned to her. "Adrianna, wilt thou have this man to be thy wedded husband, to live together after God's ordinance, in the holy estate of matrimony? Wilt thou obey him and serve him, love, honor, and keep him in sickness and in health; and forsaking all others, keep thee only unto him, so long as ye both shall live?"

"I will," whispered Adrianna.

"Who giveth this woman to be married to this man?"

"I do," Sam Atherton said, and he gave her right hand to Jonathan who placed it in Foy's.

With Foy's strong handclasp, Adrianna's fear vanished. Steadily, she pledged her troth and smiled at him as he slipped the ring on her finger. He received her ring.

Jonathan was praying, joining their right hands, intoning, "What therefore God hath joined together, let not man put asunder. I pronounce that Foy and Adrianna are man and wife in the name of the Father, and of the Son, and of the Holy Ghost. Amen." Jonathan smiled. "You may now kiss your bride."

Foy lifted the veil covering her face and folded it back. Their eyes met. Whispering, "Mrs. Edwards," he bent toward her lips, and she met his kiss. Cheers and congratulations, then hugs and kisses overwhelmed the happy couple and swept them into the dining room.

Ceremonially, Foy unsheathed his naval sword and handed it to Adrianna. Her arms shook as she lifted the long sword. Foy's strong hands closed over her delicate fingers, strengthening her as together they cut the first slice of cake. Laughing, she fed the rich cake to Foy.

For the formal wedding portrait, they moved to the mahogany secretary where Foy sat in a stiff-backed chair with his arm propped on the small desk. Adrianna stood slightly behind.

Poof! The photographer's black powder went off with an acrid smell and a blinding flash.

"Fire," a coarse voice yelled. "Mr. Foy, Mr. Foyeee!" Lige tumbled into the back hall. "Yo' warehouse a'fire!"

twelve

Adrianna stood unmoving as Foy kissed her and ran after Lige. As news of the fire rippled across the room, all the men rushed out.

Adrianna tried to smile and move graciously among the ladies who stood about chattering nervously. Lily whispered for her to cut souvenir pieces of the wedding cake for the guests. Although Lily tried to keep her movements from looking like she was sending the guests away, Adrianna sensed her tension.

Old Mrs. Robbins followed Adrianna about giving her streams of advice on marriage. "Now let me show you how to seal up a piece of cake to keep for wedding anniversaries." she said. "I still had crumbs to feed my husband on our golden wedding day."

Clanging bells interrupted her spiel. Everyone rushed to the window. The E.B. Youngs were assembling.

Another fire alarm bell rang. "That's the signal for the Chattahoochee Number 5," said Emma in a hushed voice. "It must be a terrible fire!"

Adrianna turned to Lily and whispered, "Oh, we must go—" Her voice broke.

"Yes," Lily agreed.

With trembling hands, Adrianna removed her veil. The grim women climbed into a buggy and headed toward the warehouses.

The smell of burning rags made Adrianna's nose twitch by the time they reached the bottom of the hill. Smoldering bales surrounded the cotton exchange.

"Oh." Adrianna turned at the small sound from Lily.

"It's the Number One warehouse—where all the best cotton is—was stored," Lily explained as she struggled to guide the jittery horse close to the fire.

The wood-shingled roof of the long, brick building blazed from both ends.

The "Toe-nails" stood staunchly dug into the wet ground as they pumped frantically. Holding the hose nozzle, Mr. Schrieber cried, "Vater, Vater, gif' me vater!"

Adrianna shrieked as she saw Foy coming out from the smoke-filled building with another bale on a hand truck. With a roar, the fire met, and the roof exploded upward, then collapsed into the thick-walled shell.

Lily's hand restrained Adrianna from running to Foy as he sat on the ground with his head in his hands. "He's all right."

"I'll never get that uniform clean," Adrianna said in a voice wavering between laughter and tears. The sudden realization that Foy's personal care was now her task sent a thrill of joy through her.

At the far end of the warehouse, she saw the Cleburne Company's new engine training its hose upon the carriage factory. Men were tiring. In the lull as they left their engines and fresh crews stepped up, fire burst out in several places.

"Oh, the wind is spreading it everywhere!" Adrianna wailed.

"There's not much wind," Lily replied flatly. "It's starting in too many places."

"You mean . . ."

Lily bit off the word, "Arson."

"No! Green?"

For a long moment they sat clutching each other's hands,

thinking of the proud man who had suffered so much indignity at the hands of their family.

"Surely not Green." Adrianna broke the silence first.

"Surely not," Lily agreed. "Green doesn't live by the same principles as my Harrison, but he does have his own code of honor. No! He couldn't have done anything this dangerous, but who can tell what he might—what he may do?"

Night was falling when the fire companies finally contained the fire. Foy's face was streaked with smut and his eyes sagged when at last he came to speak to Adrianna.

"We've controlled the spreading." He smiled and winked. "Go on home and bid our guests good-night. I'll be there soon."

"Home," Adrianna whispered. She blew a kiss gently toward him.

Barbour Hall was empty at last. Well-wishers, friends, dish washers, all were gone. Adrianna stretched in the cool emptiness of the marble-floored hall. The heavy perfume of roses filled her with longing. She picked up an extravagant bouquet of yellow roses and climbed the stairs, loving each step possessively. She placed the roses on the marbletop table beside the massive bed in the master bedroom. Dreamily, she untied the wine velvet curtains from the straight walnut bedposts which held aloft a thronelike canopy.

Carefully laying aside her wedding gown, she lavished her French hyacinth perfume on her pulsepoints and slipped into a white nightgown of delicately embroidered linen. She sighed in pure happiness. Everything was the perfection she had always imagined for her wedding night.

Bam! The front door slammed and footsteps clattered across the hall.

"Wife! Where are you?"

"Here," she called, running to look over the balcony rail.

Foy's face had been scrubbed. He bounded up the stairs, and she flew to meet him halfway. On the landing, he smothered her with kisses, then held her back to drink in her beauty.

"My wife, my wife," he whispered. Scooping her up in his arms, he carried her up the remaining steps and over the threshold. Gently, he closed the door.

Adrianna awakened smiling. Foy's long arms were wrapped tightly about her. Shifting slightly, she lay watching him. When he stirred, she playfully kissed his ear, and he grabbed her, tussling, nuzzling.

Thus began the pattern of September. Adrianna felt no lack of a honeymoon trip. Reveling in being together, she and Foy rode through the woodland, picnicking, swimming, boating.

Suddenly, September days grew short. Work was calling Foy. Adrianna polished Barbour Hall until it shone to match the radiance of her face. Foy bounded back into the house at every possible moment, eager to enjoy their peaceful home. Only when he encountered Monsieur Le Franc, did he frown.

"Shush, he'll hear you," Adrianna forestalled his complaints. "You can't rush art. Besides, the guest room has a private entrance on the back—"

"I hate having another man in the house," Foy grumbled. "And you never did tell me what he's charging."

Adrianna bit her lip. She was beginning to worry, to tell the Frenchman the walls and ceilings had reached perfection, but he kept insisting upon one more rosebud here or apple there.

Adrianna was shocked when at last Mr. Le Franc produced his bill. She was afraid to show it to Foy. Surely he would have more money soon. Work had begun intruding upon their long, lovely nights.

More and more often Adrianna waited alone in the big bed or read by the fire smoldering on the bedroom hearth. Noisily Foy would appear, declaring, "You'll never make a fire that way. You're too stingy with the fat li'dard." Swiftly he would poke the aromatic splinters beneath the smoking logs. With a crackling roar, the fire would light his face as he turned to take her in his arms.

Smiling secretly, Adrianna knew she had no need of lightwood. The whole house became warm and bright the moment Foy entered.

Warm, dry days meant harvest. Wagons loaded with cotton bales squeaked and groaned their way into Eufaula. Foy was kept busy sampling and grading.

Since southern ladies had worked diligently as volunteer nurses during the war, it was now acceptable for them to take paying jobs in a few respectable positions. Adrianna begged to be allowed to help at the Cotton Exchange, but Foy, like most men, still thundered, "No wife of mine will ever work!" Yet he rationed out the money for her household expenses.

With hours to spend alone, Adrianna turned to her painting. The brilliant blue of the cloudless October sky drew her to the belvedere one day and out to the garden the next.

On a Sunday afternoon so beautiful she had begged to go for a drive, Foy had left to work at something he said could not wait. Wandering listlessly in the garden, Adrianna paused to watch a pair of cardinals twittering together in a weigela bush. Summer's last trumpet-shaped blooms nearly matched the scarlet birds they encircled.

Excitedly Adrianna made a thumbnail sketch, working swiftly to get her values right. Cadmium red mixed with just a touch of alizarin crimson seemed perfect. Quickly, she wet her paper and carried it to her easel in the garden. Striving to keep her work transparent, she put in the lighter parts of the bush, let the first work dry, then stroked in the darker stems. Letting out her breath, she sat back smiling, waiting for the precise moment to paint in the crimson blossoms.

"Adrian-na," Lily's voice called from the porch.

Adrianna hated to be stopped before her creation was complete. "Here," she called grudgingly. The frightened birds flew to the top of a pine tree. "Come around here, Lily."

"Oh, there you are." Lily rounded a turning in the path. "I'd hoped to see you two at church this morning. Don't you think it's about time you—"

"We'll go when we get older," Adrianna said crossly. "We're too busy now." She reached out with a wet, shaking brush and her colors ran, obscuring the brown female. There was no way to save it, so she tried to take advantage of the accident by swirling in a few dead leaves.

"You've really become very good," said Lily sincerely. "You could have painted the friezes in the dining room yourself."

"I almost wish I had." Adrianna sighed. "I might have done the stenciling, but I'm not nearly good enough for the free hand flowers Mr. Le Franc painted."

"Is he finished?"

"Yes," she replied tersely.

She turned to face Lily but looked beyond her to the house. Narrowing her eyes at the peeling white paint and shabby green shutters, she spoke in a chilly voice. "I have no more workmen engaged except to paint the outside of the house."

Lily nodded at the obvious need, then said slowly, "I came through the back hall. Mama's sofa—her most treasured piece—I should have mentioned to you sooner about giving things away. I hope you didn't—the S-shaped legs were made for only a period of about ten years, around 1783. Besides sentiment, it was *quite* valuable."

"I know. I didn't give it away. I sold it."

The two women sat so silently that the birds returned.

"Honestly, Lily," Adrianna said miserably. "I didn't know I was spending more than Foy had. He won't tell me things. All of this," she said, waving her hand, "seemed limitless to me. He let me go on and on spending before he exploded about having no liquid assets." She pressed her trembling lips together and admitted, "I dismissed Mr. Le Franc. I sold the couch to pay him."

Pain played over Lily's face. When at last she spoke, her voice shook. "I understand. I was afraid you two weren't happy."

"We're fine," snapped Adrianna. Defiance melting, she spoke wistfully, "Do you really think I'm good? Could I sell some paintings?"

"Perhaps," said Lily kindly. "But I'm afraid that nothing we do will bring in enough money to help. Being patient will help the most. I know you get lonely with Foy working such long hours. I miss Harrison, too. He's been gone so much on the *Mignonne*. But remember, dear," she said gently, "they're doing it for us—trying to get their business going again."

Adrianna made no reply.

"Harrison usually tells me everything. We had our problems before we married because of his humility and my parents' pride, but we worked things out before the marriage—which is the best way to prevent mistakes. Of course, *we* had the same values."

Adrianna capped and uncapped her tube of paint.

"Harrison and I have been through some hard times, but always we've had each other to depend on."

Adrianna still did not reply. Lily rose to leave.

"Foy and I have always been close," Lily said softly. "I know how much he loves you, and I want to help you. But there's something bothering Foy that you and I don't know about. I've an uneasy feeling . . ." Lily shivered, was gone.

Adrianna sat staring at her painting. She longed for the kind of lasting relationship Lily and Harrison had, but she didn't know how to reach for it. Remembering the chilly echoes of her childhood home and the fearful time when her father had gone away for good, Adrianna shivered.

"Pretty, pret-ty, pret-ty," the cardinal sang over her head.

"Am I only *pretty* to him?" she asked the bird. If Foy loved her only when she did right, she could not survive. Making unending mistakes, she seemed to be her own worst enemy.

Sadly, she picked up her brush and added the focal point of her painting. Determined not to stop again before she finished, she ignored Foy's horse clattering up the driveway. She heard Foy moving through the house, banging doors. Stroking slowly, deliberately, she continued to paint until she felt him behind her, glaring at her work.

"You let the fire go out in the stove," Foy complained. "A dutiful wife would have—"

"A dutiful wife?" Adrianna exploded. "You think I should have waited and waited and sat there poking in wood—"

"I know. I'm late—again," Foy admitted ruefully. He came up behind her and hugged her close. "Have you got anything good? I'm starved."

Adrianna twisted away and went into the kitchen. She brought out tepid food from the pie safe. Silently, she sat beside him watching him wolf down congealed peas and clammy corn bread.

Foy gave her a lopsided grin. "Did you have a lonely afternoon? I had to get my books straightened out while everything was quiet." He reached for a second helping. "Cotton will be pouring in tomorrow. This is the first really big crop since the war."

"I'd have rather been alone." She picked at a crumb. "Lily came scolding." She lifted clouded eyes to his serious face. "You'll be getting enough cotton to pay your bills, then?"

"Well." He sighed. "It doesn't work that way. Right now I'm buying cotton. You see, a cotton broker buys from farmers. I warehouse it until I can resell, and—I might as well tell you—my fire insurance hasn't been renewed."

Adrianna looked at him blankly, "Have you tried another company?"

"The only other agency in town is owned by Green Bethune."

"Oh," she replied absently. "Will he be coming back? Maybe he could take my water colors to New York to sell—"

"You stay away from Green." An unaccustomed arrogance twisted Foy's lip. "I can afford to finance your little painting."

"Finance my little painting!" Adrianna erupted. She stamped into the kitchen and threw the dirty dishes into the dishpan, breaking two.

Cold fury sealed Adrianna's lips as she and Foy went about preparations for the night. Without a word, she took her pillow and started from the master bedroom.

"What're you doing?" Foy gripped her wrist.

"I don't want to sleep in here tonight," she flared. She withdrew her hand, and her chin jutted out. "I'll try Lily's old bed tonight."

"Well just maybe," he shouted. "Maybe I'll rest more in my old room."

Staring at the spider-web patterns cast by the moonlight through the macramé canopy of Lily's bed, Adrianna lay shivering miserably. The nighttime temperature had suddenly dropped, and she felt as cold, lonely, and unloved as she had in childhood. She had been a bride for one beautiful month. Scrubbing at tear-wet cheeks, she thought that her honeymoon was over. Had her marriage also ended?

Far into the night, Adrianna tossed and turned. She went to the window and looked out at a spectacular harvest moon. The beauty of silhouetted branches filled her with excitement. Here was another moment of time she must capture and preserve for those who looked but did not see. Foy thought her painting was something with which she frittered away time. Art meant everything to her, and she must make him understand.

She tiptoed into his room. Sprawled diagonally across the bed, Foy snored in exhausted sleep. There was no room for her.

Creeping back to the front room, Adrianna gazed out the window. She had sensed a growing professional quality about her work which Lily had confirmed. She would sell some paintings and have money she didn't have to beg for. *I'll show Mr. Foy he won't have to finance my little painting*, she thought bitterly. She climbed into bed and cried herself to sleep.

Throughout the week, Adrianna remained red-eyed and Foy went about in a daze. Although they had kissed and made up one night, by daylight they seemed more and more estranged. Foy's moroseness made Adrianna fear his love for her had run its course.

A respite came from an unexpected source. Low water kept the *Mignonne* stranded. Since Lily had made the trip with Harrison, Adrianna merely had to cope with a worried husband.

She busied herself supervising the painting of the house. Peeling white paint was scraped away. Adrianna watched with pleasure as the workmen smoothed burnt sienna on the walls of the spreading house.

The sun was straight overhead before she realized it, and Foy appeared for dinner.

"Brown!" He exploded. "You're painting Mama's house *brown*?"

"I like it," Adrianna said coolly. "Besides, I thought it was my—our home now."

Foy ducked his head sheepishly. "It is. I'm sorry. But—*brown*?"

"Wait 'til it's finished," she pleaded. "The shutters will be a darker, richer brown and the dental trim and up there around the belvedere will be light cream. It will set off the architectural details."

Foy frowned. "I don't know. Lily always said she looked like a belle dressed for a ball, and—"

"Well, she's an old dowager now, and brown velvet suits her—and me." Suddenly her temper flared. "I doubt there's anything in your precious Bible that says a house has to be white!"

Foy winced. "Adrianna, don't be flippant." He reached for her hand. "I should have been a better witness. Lily told me I should lead you to become a Christian before we married. I understand her reasoning now. With so many new things to adjust to . . ."

"I'm just as good as you are." She jerked her hand away. "I was raised by the Ten Commandments."

"Of course you're a good person, darling," Foy said, trying to put his arms around her. "But being good and following the Commandments doesn't save us from our sins. We are saved by grace through faith in Christ, and—don't you remember how the rich young ruler went away sorrowful?"

"I don't know what you're talking about. But don't call me a sinner," she snapped. She turned away coldly. "You'll have to get something to eat at Rowlett's. I'm busy."

She felt a pang of guilt as Foy left without another word. While she was not hungry, she knew that Foy was accustomed to his biggest meal at noon. Remorseful, she spent the afternoon making his favorite pie. With cheeks red from the heat of the wood stove and hair plastered to her forehead, she carried the pie across the porch from the separate kitchen and entered the house. As she stepped into the back of the hall, her hands shook. The pie dipped, slid. Suddenly the whole thing splattered on the black and white marble floor.

At that moment a face appeared at the front entrance. "Hello," the woman called cheerily. "I'm Mrs. Williams, Foy's Sunday school teacher."

Adrianna paced the garden. She had obviously hurt the well-intentioned visitor by snapping that she was not in the mood to attend church, but that had been nothing compared to the scene when Lily arrived and repeated Foy's words, "You've painted Mama's house *brown*?"

Wringing her hands, she felt that she could never do the things needed to please Foy's family. She could not please Foy enough to make him love her. Neither could she go back to her grandparents and admit her marriage was a failure.

Collapsing into a wicker chair in the gazebo, she dropped her face in her hands, sobbing. A heavy footstep lifted her hopes and she held out her hand. "Oh, Foy, I—"

"You're much too beautiful to cry," drawled a familiar voice. "Tell me what's the matter."

Taking both her hands in his, Green Bethune knelt before her.

thirteen

"Green!" Adrianna tried to withdraw from his grasp.

Green kissed her hands tenderly before he released her. Raking out a fine linen handkerchief, he dabbed at her tear-splotched face.

Fresh sobs shook her with the fear that Foy would find them.

"Tell ole Green what's the matter. Is the honeymoon over so soon?" He cocked his head to one side, and his blue eyes began to glitter devilishly.

"Are you ready to come away with me and see the world?"

Adrianna blew her nose on the proffered handkerchief. Frightened, she called up every shred of poise her grandmother's training had instilled.

"Not at all, Mr. Bethune." She lifted her chin as regally as Isadora and conveyed a coolness which put distance between them.

Green's assurance faltered, but he sat down, uninvited. He stroked his mutton-chop whiskers and watched her.

"Every bride must shed a few tears." She managed a smile and spoke as brightly as possible. "What are you doing in—the country?"

Green's features relaxed into sincerity as he said, "I had to see you again. To be sure before I returned to New York." He leaned toward her, reaching out.

Adrianna stopped him with stiff-backed reserve. "Oh, you're going to New York? Would you do me a favor?"

"Anything."

"Could you take some of my watercolors? Perhaps my old teachers would display them, and maybe . . ."

"Sell them?" He finished for her. "You need money, then?" He slid his hand inside his expensively tailored jacket. "Let me—"

"No, no!" she said quickly before he could bring out his wallet. "I'd like to become established as an artist, that's all, Lily thinks I'm good enough—and . . ." Suddenly she slumped, defeated. "Yes, I do need money. I've run up too many bills to present a new husband." She tossed her head as again he reached inside his coat. "No, I couldn't accept a loan from you, but if you'd take the paintings . . ."

"Consider it done, fair lady. But have you thought about your insurance policy?"

"What about it?"

"You can use your insurance policy as collateral for a loan."

"Oh, really?" Adrianna clapped her hands delightedly.

Green leaned forward. "You see, you still need me to be your friend. Put on your hat, and I'll take you to the hotel for tea. When you're feeling better, I'll introduce you to my agent . . ."

"Green, thank you for your help. I'm very glad you're no longer angry with me, but . . ." Adrianna stood and held out her hand in a gesture of dismissal. "A married woman cannot, must not, try to carry on a casual friendship with another man."

Green started to protest.

Striving to be pleasant yet firm, Adrianna touched a finger to his lips and said, "No, Green, I love my husband very much, but even the most happily married woman could not allow herself to be around a man of such irresistible charm as you."

Gravely, Green clasped her fingers to his lips. He left without a word.

Adrianna realized, too late, that she still clutched his handkerchief.

Excited at the prospect of having money to pay the painters, she hurried upstairs and washed her tear-streaked face. Rinsing out the embroidered handkerchief, she laid it over the silver faucets to dry. She would leave it at the insurance office.

Dressing hurriedly, she began a frantic search for the forgotten policy. At last she found it. She was already downtown when she remembered she had left Green's monogrammed handkerchief on the lavatory.

fourteen

Foy rubbed his neck as he unfolded his long frame from the leather couch in his office. It had been a miserable night.

I behaved like an idiot, he moaned to himself. From the moment he had found Green Bethune's handkerchief, he had ranted and raved. He believed Adrianna's tearful explanation, but he had reeled from the blow to his pride. Anger seared him again as he thought of how she had told his worst enemy she needed money instead of confessing it to him.

Balling his pillow and afghan to throw them into a chest, Foy jerked around and saw a grinning Green Bethune.

"New housing accommodations, I see."

"Uh." Foy cleared his throat. "Working late and fell asleep," he muttered. "Gotta sell cotton, you know. You buying today?"

Green smiled sardonically.

Shifting uncomfortably in the malignant silence, Foy waited.

Green stroked the back of his hand along his whiskers. When at last he spoke, his voice was low. "I think you know. I'm here to call in our bet."

Foy snorted. "What I recall is a casual conversation—a declaration of faith in my wife. Which, by the way, hasn't changed."

He tried to turn away, but Green's piercing blue eyes held him.

"What I recall, sir, is a definite wager. I asked, 'What will you wager on whom the fair Adrianna will be to wife?'" He jerked his thumb toward where Foy had stowed his bedding. "I remember your exact words." He mocked. "'She'll marry me and that right soon. I'd stake my life. Anything. The *Mignonne Wingate.*'"

Foy struggled for control. "But surely you jest. A little tiff doesn't—"

"A man's word is his bond, sir." Adopting the manner which charmed the unwary, Green laughingly said, "I wouldn't simply *take* the *Mignonne Wingate.* I prefer racing—and high stakes." Suddenly he leaned down with palms flat on Foy's desk. "I'll give you a sporting chance. We'll set up a race. If the *Mignonne* is fast enough to rendezvous with my ship, we're square. If not, she's mine. That is, if she survives the trip. If not, I wouldn't want her anyway."

Foy opened his mouth to refuse, but Green continued.

"Let's make it interesting. See how many bales you can carry. Since you need money, I'll double the price per pound on the day you deliver. I do want the fair Adrianna properly fed. Of course, we'll let the lady herself decide which of us —"

Furious, Foy spoke between clenched teeth. "I have faith in my wife and my steamboat. What are your exact terms?"

Foy covered the distance to Barbour Hall in long strides like a horse running for the barn. His mind galloped faster still as he moved from wounded pride at Green's discovery of his problems to despair at the thought of losing the boat for which he had worked so long. Too agitated to tell Adrianna, he greeted her gruffly.

Sunday dinner with Lily's family could not be avoided.

Harrison served the roast beef and discoursed on local businessmen building a cotton mill in Eufaula.

"Of course, it's the thing to do," he said, "but I'm afraid too many have returned from the war with nothing but missing limbs and tattered uniforms. I don't know where the ten or eleven years have gone since the war, but I expect it will be ten more before they can raise enough capital to buy spindles and looms."

Foy mumbled a noncommittal sound.

Harrison eyed his morose guests but kept talking. "John Tullis and the Lampley brothers are shipping more cotton to New England mills, but don't you think we'd best keep shipping directly to Liverpool?"

Foy said nothing.

Lily looked at the blanched faces around her table and tried to bridge the conversational gap. "I don't know how you all ever know what to do about selling with the price so low and the constant fluctuations." She stood up to begin clearing the table.

"I know a way we can get double the price." Foy's voice echoed in his ears. "From Green."

"Is he back? I wish he'd stay in South Carolina!" Lily clanked the silver in the plate. "He doesn't ever quite break laws, but he shaves principles," she continued. "Don't deal with Green!"

As if that settled it, she picked up the platter and started to the butler's pantry. Adrianna and Mignonne followed with the plates.

"Lily," Adrianna said hesitantly, "do you want that canopy bed in your old room? Grandfather is sending me a modern one."

"Yes, I'd like it for Mignonne," Lily replied. "It's a

Sheraton. I always loved that room because the morning sun pours in."

Hearing Lily through the open doorway, Foy's face burned because the concern in Lily's voice told him that Kitty had gossiped. Lily knew they had moved from the master bedroom.

Not catching the meaning Foy had, Adrianna spoke glumly. "I promise not to dispose of any more of your mother's things. Green took some of my paintings to sell, and—"

"Have you been seeing Green?" Lily's voice shrilled. "I was wondering if Foy were sick or mad. Here, Mignonne, take the scuppernong cobbler to the dining room to dip."

Foy ducked his head as the girl brought in the pie. The women's voices, echoing against the crockery in the hall-like pantry, became angrier.

"It was just a petty argument. Green came looking for Foy on business, and . . ." Suddenly, she shouted, "Of course, I'm not seeing Green. I may not understand your precious Bible, but . . . but . . . ," she spluttered. "I'm good enough to be true to my husband." She began to cry. "Even—" She snatched a sob. "Even if he leaves me."

Suddenly the narrow passage was filled with bewildered faces.

"What's going on?" demanded Harrison sternly.

"She accused me of seeing Green!" Adrianna buried her face against Foy's chest.

Foy stood stiff-armed. "She's not seeing Green," he said in a cold monotone. "But how did he know . . ." He backed away from her. "That you moved out of my bedroom?"

"I don't know." She sobbed harder.

Lily tried to shoo the children outdoors. Beau scampered out, but Mignonne obstinately remained.

"Green knew plenty. He came snooping at the office early this morning." Foy threw out his arms. "Y'all will have to know. He caught me sleeping at the office. He'd goaded me into saying something and . . . Well, Green's called in a bet." Foy dropped his head in his hands. "He says I no longer have you 'to wife' so I forfeit a wager I made. He says we have to win a race with the *Mignonne* or lose her."

"You risked my namesake?" squealed the dark-haired girl.

"How could you doubt me?" Adrianna's fiery mane flew wildly with her rage.

Foy jutted his chin at her. "That was the problem. I thought I could depend on you."

Mignonne tugged at his arm and shrieked, "No, no, you can't! Papa! Stop him!"

Distractedly, Foy shook her off and faced Adrianna. "I thought I could depend on you. In this family we believe 'What God hath joined together let no man put asunder'."

"Maybe God hasn't joined us," Adrianna flung out the words and shrank back into a corner, weeping.

"Now, now." Harrison waved his hands in a calming gesture. "Quiet down, all of you. A race might be great sport. We have a fine craft. I, for one, would like to see what she can do."

"You can't condone a race!" exploded Lily. "The Chattahoochee is too narrow for two boats! The rocks— No! It's too dangerous!"

"Dangerous, yes." Harrison tilted his head boyishly. "But not impossible. Two boats can't race side by side, but there are other ways to race. Let Foy talk."

Relieved at Harrison's attitude, Foy felt his blood flowing again. "The race will be against time and the obstacles in the river. Green has it all figured out: how fast a time we must make, how many bales we must carry. We'll have check points."

"We'll turn his trick to our advantage!" Harrison rubbed his hands together exultantly. "Just think what good publicity this will be. If we're the fastest, it will help us get business, Lily." He grinned sheepishly. "If steamboats are to compete with all these new railroads, we must increase our speed and improve our ability to keep to a schedule."

"We're to leave Thursday morning. If we meet Green's ship at Apalachicola Bay before it leaves for Liverpool at dawn on Saturday, he'll pay *double* the going rate for the cotton. You've got to take some risks in life or lose everything." Foy shot a meaningful glance at Adrianna who still cowered in the corner.

"Are you saying we'll lose..." Mignonne's lip trembled.

"I know it's not fair to you, but he didn't give me much choice. If we don't make it in time," Foy mumbled without looking at his niece, "Green will get our steamboat."

Mignonne began to shriek again.

"You must stop this, Harrison," Lily demanded against the din.

"Now, Lily, I know only too well how Green can get a fellow involved in something he doesn't want to do."

"But, but—" Lily sobbed. "Nobody's ever raced on the Chattahoochee. Least if they did, they didn't live to tell the tale!"

fifteen

Uhmmmmm! Uhmmmmm!

The steamboat's whistle floated up the Columbus, Georgia, street, grating Adrianna's nerves. She wanted to run away, yet she must be a part of this foolhardy race.

Adrianna tried to lengthen her strides to keep up with Lily, but her slim skirt restricted her. She glanced gratefully at her sister-in-law. Against the men's protests, Lily had declared the women would face the trip with them no matter what the dangers.

Lily's brown eyes still flashed with anger, but her springing step bespoke excitement as she glanced over her shoulder.

"Emma, Emma, come quickly," Lily sang out. "We stayed far too long settling the children with Aunt Laurie."

"I don't—hurry as fast as I used to," Emma puffed. Smiling at Adrianna's taut face, she spoke reassuringly, "Everything will be all right."

Uhmmmmm! Uhmmmmm!

The rousing blast drew them down to the wharf where the steamboat, emitting black puffs of smoke, quivered as a thing alive.

Wheet! Wheet! From the lofty pilothouse, Foy saluted them with the whistle.

Harrison paced the deck with his watch in his hand. Excitedly, he swung the watch chain fastened to his belt as he spoke. "It's nearly time to leave. We've lightened the load all we can." He grinned and brushed back his graying temples. "I even got a haircut."

Adrianna laughed and matched his frivolous tone. "Well, I'm traveling light. I left my trunk. Do you believe I can survive with just one frock? Can't I take two?" She glanced at the steamer's furniture which had been moved to the wharf. "You've made me plenty of room."

Everyone laughed and started on their separate ways. Crossing the empty freight deck, Adrianna went to the upper deck and squeezed past burlap-wrapped cotton which arrogantly crowded what was normally passenger space. When this race was over, she would go back to her mother, but for now she continued to climb toward Foy.

Singing called Adrianna's attention to the banks. In astonishment, she saw a huge crowd along the riverfront and watching from the upper windows of the Columbus Iron Works. Green Bethune's agent strutted up and down the steep roadway like a cock of the walk.

Bong! Bong! A clock struck. Bong! Adrianna ran up the remaining steps to the pilothouse. Bong! Friday, Bong! November 3. Bong! 1876. Bong! Eight o'clock. Bonggg!

As the last note reverberated on the misty air, Harrison saluted Green's man. Gangplanks fell upon the hardened deck. Lines let go. With a deep, hoarse puff, the *Mignonne Wingate* swung back and shot straight from her mooring. Green's man stared at the watch in his hand and his jaw fell.

Foy chortled. "We gained three minutes on his time already. He thought we'd back outstream."

"I wish we didn't have to stop to load at Eufaula," said Adrianna. "I understand that you want to top off the load where the water is deeper, but as long as it took us to get to the bay before, I don't see how we'll ever make it from here by Saturday dawn."

"Well," said Foy, "If I hadn't lost so much cotton in the fire, we would have had three thousand bales in the warehouse. But Green probably would've demanded we load some at Columbus, anyway, since it's the head of navigation." He shrugged.

Ahead, the morning fog seemed to be an impenetrable wall. Adrianna could barely see the river. As she strained her eyes to see, Adrianna remembered tales of fiery wrecks and lost lives. Not wanting to distract Foy and feeling too estranged to sit quietly beside him, Adrianna wandered to the ladies' saloon.

Lily sat with a big book in her lap. Beside her lay a Bible and two books by Charles Darwin. She looked up and laughed as Adrianna entered. "If Harrison saw these books, he'd say I'm making the boat draw more than its allowed twenty-two inches." She patted the velvet settee beside her in invitation for Adrianna to join her. "Adrianna, I'm afraid I've been dogmatic with you. I realized I needed to read all this and do what I've told you—think for myself."

Adrianna sat on the edge of the couch and glanced at the geology time scale Lily tapped with her finger.

"Way before Darwin, the English geologist Lyell named these eras. Look." She spread the Bible open to Genesis. "The Bible doesn't suppose to be a science book, but amazingly, it gives the order of creation, plants, fish and fowl, then mammals, exactly as recently discovered."

"Umm-huh."

"I wouldn't find too much disagreement with *Origin of the Species* if Darwin hadn't cut out, 'In the beginning God,' but . . ."

Adrianna did not really care. When the race was over, she would move in with her mother who pressed her only on the most trivial matters.

Lily raised her voice and pulled at Adrianna's arm to claim her attention. "But when I tried to wade through *The Descent of Man*, I was upset by how Darwin tried to explain away God Himself."

The cluck, cluck of the waterwheel slowed to a swish, swish.

"Citing ways he thinks animals are just as good as man, Darwin tries to explain away the fact that people feel God in their hearts and have morals, duty to one another."

Not seeming to notice the boat's lack of progress, Lily continued. "Of course, God can create through any means He chooses, but personally, I see it the way Archbishop Whately tried to point out: Man came into the world a civilized being; savages have undergone degradation just as nations have fallen away in civilization, lapsing into barbarism."

"Yes, I see what you mean." Adrianna nodded.

"I pray for Mrs. Darwin. I feel so sorry for her."

"Why?" Adrianna looked startled.

"She is well known to be a Christian. She must have been proud of her husband's scientific thinking in the beginning, but how it must pain her that he now declares himself agnostic!"

"What does that mean?"

"One who says he doesn't know about God because he can't prove Him."

"But we can't prove God," Adrianna exclaimed.

"We don't need to," said Lily. "He proves us. We can *feel* God's love filling our souls, *see* it demonstrated in the lives of true believers, *taste* it in the glories of nature."

Bam! The boat stopped with a groaning of wood. Precariously balanced, Adrianna hit the floor.

Lily helped her up and they ran to the deck.

"Whew!" Harrison blew out his cheeks. "We're in a stretch of low water," he said grimly. "Grounded on a sandbar."

"But Lily," Adrianna plucked her sleeve. "I thought that was why we left Columbus with a light load—because of low water."

"Yes, dear," Lily said soothingly. "We'll top off the load at Eufaula because the water is usually better there. This is just one of those things that happen."

They leaned over the rail to watch. Men jumped off on the white sand and began to shovel it away from the boat. Others grabbed long poles and tried to push the boat from the bar.

Precious minutes pounded away.

"Oh, Lily, what—"

Lily shook her head resignedly. "Sometimes we can only sit for a freshet, a rain upstream which makes the river rise."

The red globe of the sun had burned away the early mists. Streaming through the trees on the Georgia shore, the sunlight cast flames through translucent maple leaves. The beauty seared Adrianna's heart as she recalled Foy's words, "Maple leaves in autumn, springtime in my heart." Overcome with weeping, she went into her stateroom and threw herself on the bunk.

Adrianna did not know how long she cried or how the steamboat got underway again. She only knew she could not face Foy's family. She lay staring at the sign on her stateroom door, "Should anything happen to the boat, remove this door and cling to it. It will float and save your life." *I need more than that*, she thought and began to weep again.

Hot sun beat on her head and dazzled her eyes when at last Adrianna emerged at four in the afternoon. Looking up at the Alabama bluffs, she could see Eufaula.

The *Mignonne* landed smartly. By prearranged plan, stevedores sprang up from the wharf and set to work loading.

A huge man sang out, "You's making mighty good time, Cap'n Harrison."

Adrianna brightened. The watch pinned to her white shirtwaist showed five o'clock when they departed from Eufaula. Her blood singing again, she ran lightly up to the pilothouse.

"Open that throttle, Mr. Murphey," Foy said into the speaking tube which connected with the engineer far below. "Keep those gauges to the top, Jonathan." He grinned at Adrianna. Wrapping his arm about her waist, he pulled her close beside him.

Watching his profile as he stared intently downriver, Adrianna thought, *he doesn't know how badly I'm hurting.*

At eight o'clock with the night turned crisp and cold, they swung into the landing at Fort Gaines, Georgia. The crew had lapsed into relaxed routine. Now every muscle tensed. Commands were shouted through megaphones. The crew shouldered cordwood waiting on the dock, and paraded back, laughing, joking.

When once again the *Mignonne Wingate* was slipping silently through the night, the family sat down to supper. Harrison pulled a small package from his pocket. "Happy anniversary." He looked adoringly at Lily as if she were a bride.

Lily kissed him soundly in spite of the watching group.

Before she opened her gift, she hurried out and returned with a cake she had smuggled aboard.

Tears misted Adrianna's eyes. She could not see the present Lily was exclaiming over. She did not taste the flavor of the cake Harrison was declaring his special favorite.

When the men had gone back to their posts, the three women went into the ladies' saloon. Adrianna cried in anguish, "Oh, Lily! I hadn't realized today was your anniversary. I'm so sorry. I've ruined everything. You'll probably lose *your* boat." She sniffed. "Maybe even our lives."

"After eighteen years, I don't need a party—but what could be more exciting than this?" Lily laughed. "Besides that, we will not lose *our* boat, and our *lives* are in God's keeping."

Adrianna bowed her bright head and spoke in muffled sobs. "You're still in love after eighteen years, and already Foy—I'm afraid he'll leave me like my father left . . ." She began to sob uncontrollably.

Lily wrapped Adrianna in her arms and stroked her hair. "Darling, I love you. We all do. Foy will never leave you."

"How can you be sure of that?" Adrianna clung to Lily.

"I know because he's a Christian. His love for you is based on his love for God. Whether we are good or bad makes no difference. God loves us. God sees infinite worth in every person He created in spite of our sin."

Adrianna stiffened, but Lily continued earnestly.

"Foy will never stop loving you and trying to do what is best for you. He will cherish you, no matter what. But we must start at the beginning. I've tried to dive into the middle, to tell you what I think you should do, and I haven't been the help I want to be."

Adrianna sniffed and scrubbed at her cheeks. She sat back and looked into Lily's concerned face.

"Long ago I gave my life to the Lordship of Christ. I've wanted to bring all my family to this wonderful joy, but . . ." she laughed ruefully. "Sometimes I'm too eager for everyone to let God's love fill their spiritual emptiness. I push too hard. But Emma . . ."

Lily paused and patted the placid woman who sat quietly beside them in an attitude of prayer.

"Emma has shown me that I needed to stop and confess my own sins."

"But you're not a sinner! Everyone talks about what a wonderful Christian you are."

"I'm a Christian because I've accepted on faith that Christ died to pay the penalty for my sin. Paul tells us that all have sinned, missed the mark of the high calling of God, and deliberately stepped over the boundaries God has set. But through God's grace—that word means unmerited favor—we are set free from our sins simply by faith in Christ Jesus. I'm sure of my salvation, my place in heaven.

"We are not saved as a reward for being good—we could never do enough good works to reconcile ourselves to God. We are saved as a gift because we are spiritually needy. To demonstrate this change we are to do good for others in the Savior's name. We must confess our daily sins and then build our lives on Christ. But wait. Let me show you."

Lily returned with her Bible and thumbed quickly to First Corinthians 3:11. " 'For other foundation can no man lay than that is laid, which is Jesus Christ. Now if any man build upon this foundation gold . . . hay, stubble . . .' " she ran her finger down the verses, " 'it shall be revealed by fire; and the fire shall try every man's work . . .' "

She looked up at Adrianna. "We're constantly tried by fire, tested, but if our lives are founded on Christ, if our marriages have this basis—"

"But if Foy would talk to me, explain—then I would . . ." Adrianna looked at her hands twisting in her lap.

"Fine, you need to talk things out. But I'm not speaking about compromise— 'I'll give in on this, if you do that.'— I mean having God's kind of love for each other. The Greek word for that is *agape*. It means *always* seeking the highest good of the other."

Adrianna sat for a long moment considering the difference. "I've never read the Bible," she admitted. "It's such a—difficult book."

"I used to think that, too," said Emma softly. "It's because the Bible came from unlimited God to limited man. You cannot understand the Bible with your natural mind as you understand philosophers. The Bible is spiritual, and you must be born of the Spirit or it will remain a difficult, closed book."

"Oh, that's too hard!"

"No, it isn't, dear. For long, painful years, I wouldn't listen to what Lily was trying to share. I attended church when I had to—as a duty. Then one day I opened my heart to God's Holy Spirit. Now I want to be in God's house every Sabbath to find peace for my soul and strength for the week ahead. I hear God speaking to me when I approach the Bible praying that the Spirit will teach me."

"Start with the Gospel of John," Lily said smiling. "It has the deepest theology, yet it's also the easiest for a beginner to understand. It will show you that sinners cannot get right with God through their own efforts. Calvary's cross was necessary."

Adrianna was rescued from having to answer the earnest women because Harrison came in to tell them that they were exactly on schedule. Feeling confident that they would easily win, the women decided to retire for the night.

Tossing fitfully, Adrianna suddenly sat upright. The steamer pitched and yawed, and it seemed the *Mignonne* would break like a matchstick.

Barefoot, Adrianna clambered to the pilothouse. She watched Foy wrestling the flopping wheel. Confused by the blackness of the night, Adrianna sensed they were crosswise, straining against the current. The *Mignonne* trembled, fought Foy, tried to turn back upstream.

Fearing to speak, Adrianna waited helplessly. At last Foy gained control and they once again headed downstream.

"Grannies! That was close!" Foy threw her a quick look over his shoulder.

"I didn't think you knew I was here."

Foy laughed. "You don't know how you fill the place with springtime—with more than just your perfume." He scooped her close for a quick kiss, then released her and held the knobs of the wheel with both hands. "I'd have hated to have lost her through stupid carelessness!"

"What happened?"

"For the past year there's been a dog chained on a bluff one mile north of Purcell's Swirl. He lets out a deep aooff when he hears a packet on the river." Foy scrubbed his arm across his sweaty brow.

"I'm sleepy, but I'm sure I wasn't dozing." He nodded at her ruefully. "I took a chance on going on even though there are no stars to steer by, but the ole hound must've broken his chain. Tonight he barked close to the water—and immediately, we hit the rapids and flung into the whirlpool."

"You need some coffee." Adrianna lifted the pot and found it empty.

"I'd sure bud love a cup, but the steward is late. He'll probably come around shortly."

"I want to get it for you myself." Adrianna ran down, stopping long enough to pull on cotton stockings and halfway button on her shoes. As she climbed back up with the steaming pot, she remembered previously thinking that Lily waited upon Harrison with slavelike devotion. She had been holding back until Foy did something equal for her. Now she absorbed the warmth of seeking another's good.

Companionably, they watched the dark water as the boat sashayed over the next six miles. When they docked at Columbia, Alabama, Adrianna was surprised at the crowd watching for them.

Foy flexed his shoulders and Adrianna massaged his neck while they waited for the crew to wood up and load supplies.

"You can bet there's someone telegraphing Green," Foy growled as they headed back into the stream. "Go back and get some rest. Things will be uneventful for awhile." He kissed her, let her go, then pulled her back for a long, stirring kiss. "Mr. Trimmer will take the watch at two," he promised.

Happier than she had been in weeks, Adrianna snuggled beneath the blankets and slept until she felt Foy's cold body climbing into the warm bed.

Adrianna awoke suddenly. Foy was gone. She had not

known when he left. Smiling, remembering, she blinked her eyes as the first light of a new day filtered into their cabin through stained glass windows. Stretching luxuriously, she roused enough to realize what had awakened her. Silence.

Her ears pricked. The stillness alarmed her. The rhythm of the paddle wheel had slowed, yet she had a sense of rushing forward.

Everyone was up. Lily stood gripping the rail.

"What?" Adrianna gasped.

Her eyes dark coals in her pale face, Lily whispered, "King's Rock."

It seemed the boat was standing still. Walls of menacing rock rushed past. Hurtling through the tunnel of their old nemesis, they dared not breathe. When they passed through, victorious, Lily uttered a thankful prayer.

As she went about her toilette preparing for the day, Adrianna remembered how carelessly she had ridden the river before. A stop had only meant an adventure at a new place. Now, every change in the sound of the machinery gave cause for alarm. Sighing, she gazed across the black water. The scene was no longer a romantic picture to paint.

A splintering crunch wrenched her around to the stern. She gaped down on the straining paddlewheel. A log entangled the paddles, bursting several of the wheel planks into jagged fragments. As she watched, men converged.

"One engine damaged beyond use, sir."

"One engine damaged beyond use, sir!" The shout was relayed to convey the message to Harrison.

Extricating the log took an hour. Then the men set to work replacing broken planks.

"The buckets can be repaired underway while we limp along on the other engine," Foy explained. "She'll just be hard to steer."

Drifting perilously for the next twenty miles, they finally reached the River Junction landing serving the nearby town of Chattahoochee, Florida. It was nine o'clock Saturday morning. The first twenty-four hours were behind them. They had covered 223 miles. In less than another twenty-four hours, they must go 146 more to keep their rendezvous at Apalachicola Bay.

When they moored at the wharf, a brass band struck up. Clapping, cheering, a crowd converged upon them with congratulations. Excitedly chattering people called their fast schedule a cannonball run.

Enthusiasm renewed, Adrianna greeted people in the crowd as she walked along the wharf to steady her legs from the constant motion of the steamboat. Spotting a kindred spirit, a young woman with fiery red hair, Adrianna smiled and spoke. "Oh, may I see your baby?"

"Of course." With a friendly smile she pulled back a pink blanket to allow Adrianna a peep at the puckered face.

"Oh, how precious! I hope I'll have one someday."

Uhh Uhh Uhmmmmm! The *Halli Belle*, a small steamer, blasted a warning call.

"Captain Brown's ready. Goodbye. Good luck," the redhead said and hurried aboard the *Halli Belle*.

Adrianna fidgeted. Time was fleeting. This was their longest stopover. At this point the murky green Chattahoochee and the muddy red Flint became one, and the mightier river was called the Apalachicola. Ahead of them was the Narrows where the *Wave* had sunk. Venomous Moccasin Slough lay waiting to meet them. Although Foy and Harrison were already congratulating themselves, Adrianna noticed that Jonathan told no jokes or funny stories.

When at last they were underway again, Adrianna paced the deck. The sun warmed away the mists of morning and promised a beautiful day. Lily sat exclaiming over flora and fauna, but Adrianna was too nervous to paint or sit still.

Not wanting to talk, she stood alone on the bow even though the wind chilled her. Black smoke and sparks showered her as they rounded a bend and caught up with the *Halli Belle*. The small steamer blocked the narrow channel. They could not pass.

Adrianna fumed. Surely their captain knew of the stakes in the race. Up river and down, people were wildly enthusiastic, pulling for them to set new records. Suddenly she realized the *Halli Belle* was racing, trying to be able to brag about outdistancing the *Mignonne*.

Landmarks slid by. They were losing valuable time. With her red hair whipping, Adrianna leaned far out from the bow like a ship's figurehead. She motioned aside the intruders.

The channel widened. Grazing the shoals, the *Mignonne* pulled even.

Gauging the distance between the two racers, Adrianna sighted the railings and beat her fist. "Jonathan fire that boiler," she muttered between clenched teeth.

The Mignonne pulled ahead, passed, took control of the channel. Blasting her whistle, she rounded a bend leaving the *Halli Belle* a puff of smoke and sparks above the treetops.

Ka-Boom. An explosion rent the air. Ka-Boom! Balls of fire shot over the trees.

Clang! Clang! The *Mignonne*'s bell echoed against the banks. Horrified, Adrianna recognized the pilot's signal for backing.

"No, no we can't go back," she screamed as the boat shivered to a stop and reversed the paddlewheel.

Flying wildly up the steps, Adrianna ran into the pilot-house and clawed at Foy's arm.

"No," she cried, "Don't go back, Foy. Someone else will come along to help." Tears streamed down her cheeks. "We'll never make up the time we've lost already. We'll lose everything."

"No, Adrianna." Foy's voice was cold as he pushed her out of his line of vision. "We won't lose the important things. Haven't you listened to what Lily's always saying about storing your treasures in heaven?"

"But—but," she blubbered.

"I knew when I met you that our values were different." His voice had a frightening, dead sound. "I let you tempt me to lie abed instead of worshipping on Sunday mornings as had always been my custom. I've let foolish pride make me strive for money every sort of way. I've risked this boat that isn't fully mine." He sighed heavily. "I won't compromise my principles again. I won't leave those people."

Foy backed the *Mignonne* around the bend. Adrianna stared at him wordlessly. The steamboat stopped. Adrianna clapped her hands over her face at the sight. Fire swept from the boiler room, consumed the racks of cordwood, leaped across the deck of the *Halli Belle*. Alarms clanged.

"Man the pumps, man the pumps!" Captain Brown shouted through his megaphone.

The deckhands turned from him in panic. Diving into the river, three burly men splashed and spluttered, trying to swim. Six others scrambled to lower a lifeboat. Not waiting for passengers, they all jumped at once, rocking, tilting, dumping themselves into the water.

Horror-stricken, Adrianna watched the *Mignonne*'s officers lower their own boat and row to the *Halli Belle*.

Rushing to Captain Brown's aid, they manned the pumps. They struggled with a pitiful stream of water against the roaring blaze. Swirling, wind-swept flames enveloped the cabin, beat them back. Captain Brown rushed into his office, ran back clutching record books and money just as the flaming door lintel fell.

Screaming people jumped overboard. The water was shallow, and they waded to dry land.

Tipping precariously, the flame-gutted *Halli Belle* laid her pilothouse into a treetop. The young pilot scrambled out onto the branches and climbed down the tree.

Numbly, Adrianna trailed Lily as she gave directions for the bedraggled passengers to be brought aboard the cotton-filled decks of the *Mignonne*.

Moaning, weeping people were laid on the mahogany dance floor of the grand saloon. Picking her way among them, Adrianna realized Harrison had concealed three with sheets.

Over the babble of voices, two men hurled curses at Captain Brown. They railed at the foolhardiness of racing until the *Halli Belle*'s thin boiler burst.

Fighting hysteria, Adrianna remembered the redhead and her baby. Joining others who searched for loved ones, she found the mother with the beautiful child sleeping peacefully in her arms.

Emma attended cuts and bruises. Jonathan worked to make those scalded by the steam as comfortable as possible. Burns were coated with flour to seal out air. Those of the *Halli Belle*'s crew and passengers who were unhurt retold the incident in strained, high-pitched voices.

Suddenly sickened, Adrianna ran outside to the rail, clutching her turning stomach.

Sobered by the accident, Foy called for less speed from the engineers, and they proceeded carefully downriver even after they had transferred their unexpected passengers to another steamer at the next landing. With the boat winding slowly through low, flat country, the family seemed to take on an unspoken resignation to failure. Adrianna became sick with inner turmoil, adamant that they must not lose.

Moccasin Slough taunted them next as it devoured the river into its fabled breaks in the channel. They entered the mouth. Gracefully as a swan, the *Mignonne* turned this way and that, easily making every point through the writhing trickle.

Adrianna knew that Mr. Trimmer would have insisted upon taking the vessel through this stretch of "dry land," but Foy did not come to comfort her. She stood on the bow with Lily and Harrison, peering into the swamp.

Adrianna sighed in relief when they reached the tail end of the slough. She claimed victory too soon. The hull of the *Barbara Lee* lay sunk in water over her boiler deck.

The *Mignonne*'s bell rang to pull alongside.

"Must we stop again?" Adrianna cried to Harrison. "Look! They're all right. Everyone's smiling and waving. Please let's go on. You people give up too easily!"

Harrison's voice, gentle yet firm, reproved her. "Adrianna, when I decided to be master of the *Mignonne*, I linked my destiny with her destiny. It is my duty to forget self in the interest of those whom I serve."

"But, but," Adrianna spluttered. "What about duty to . . ." Her voice rose angry. "To us?"

"Adrianna!" Lily broke in. "This is what I've been trying to tell you about Darwin."

"What?" Adrianna exploded. "Why on earth are you bringing up his name at a time like this?"

"His name is linked—perhaps unfairly—with Social Darwinism in business: the competitive struggle, the survival of the fittest. What you would have us do just now."

Adrianna stared at her wild-eyed.

"I don't pretend to understand pragmatism and all of the other 'isms' which draw people in all directions," Lily said flatly. "But I know that to say 'whatever works is good and true' is wrong. God is unchangeable truth. It is not right to do the wrong thing for what you consider the right reasons. The Bible clearly sets forth good and evil, right and wrong."

Face perspiring, cheeks flaming, Adrianna felt suddenly cold inside. "Your fundamentals—your precious principles—" She choked. "Are they more important than losing the *Mignonne* to Green?"

"Of course. Our defeats are merely punctuation, commas in God's plan for us. Let Green have his money and power. What we have is . . ."

Adrianna fled.

Flinging herself upon her bed, she wept her misery. How Foy and his family must hate her! Everything was all her fault.

Persistent knocking at her cabin door penetrated her sobs. Foy and Lily called, pleaded. She would not let them in.

Darkness fell. Everything seemed lost.

sixteen

The smothering blackness of the night merged with the darkness in Adrianna's soul. None of them would ever forgive her. There was nothing to do but leave. She had taken so many wrong avenues, thinking she had plenty of time to find her way. Now, totally alone, she had completely lost direction.

She slipped to the floor. Bowing her head on her bunk, she began to speak aloud. "They can't forgive me. But if you'll forgive me, God, *only* if you'll forgive me, can I live! I told Foy I was not a sinner. Now I know I am, and I can't redeem myself."

Repentant, Adrianna confessed all the sins of mind and heart in her young life and turned away from all she had been seeking.

Her sobbing ceased. The turbulent raging within her quieted. The blackness of midnight wrapped her in a warm, velvet blanket with its blessing of rest. The room seemed filled with the person, power, and presence of God.

"Oh, dear Jesus," she prayed. "Now I know You are alive! I thankfully accept the gift of Your loving sacrifice for me."

Knowing that God's love would go with her no matter what happened, she stopped trembling. She lit her lamp and thumbed to the Gospel of John in the Bible Lily had given her.

" 'In the beginning was the Word.' " She smiled. The Holy Spirit was already helping her to understand. *The*

Word is Jesus. " 'In him was life; and the life was the light of men.' " She read through the fourteenth chapter. " 'I am the way, the truth, and the life: no man cometh unto the Father, but by me.' "

Wonder filled her. She had questioned how to find truth. Now she saw that she must begin with truth, Jesus Christ, and not deter from that. She had searched everywhere for a guide for her life. The Bible had been right here at her fingertips.

As God's voice spoke to her from the pages of the Bible, Adrianna knew she would never again withdraw from those she loved. The love bubbling up within her needed to be shared. She must see Foy.

Quickly, she washed her face and brushed her red hair. With her hand on the door, she turned back and lavished on the scent of hyacinth. Her delicate face sparkled in a confident smile as she climbed the stairs to the starlit glass house.

"Hello, I'm Adrianna Atherton." Her rising inflection transmitted her smile. Her voice dropped low as she added sincerely, "But I want to be Adrianna Edwards."

Foy turned. The painfully serious set of his face lifted as a slow smile appeared. He doffed his braided cap, bowed low, and intoned, "Foy Edwards, Esquire, at your service ma'am." His dark eyes twinkled and his firm mouth twitched mischievously. He wrapped his arms around her and pulled her close beside him at the wheel.

"I love you. I was in love with you before we met." He nuzzled her fragrant hair. "You'll be Adrianna Edwards, always and forever." He sealed his words with a fervent kiss.

Trembling with the wonder that Foy's God-given love had continued even when she had gone astray, Adrianna nestled in the warmth of his arms.

"I'm so sorry, Foy. I've been awful—but tonight I've

committed my heart to Christ's lordship. From now on I'll base my life and our marriage on His love."

Foy hugged her so tightly that she laughingly protested the safety of her ribs.

"One thing though." She pushed back to look at him. "Please talk to me. Explain. I was only spending money like my family has always lived. I don't really care about money, but make me understand."

"I'm sorry. I've been as wrong as you. Pride got in my way. Adrianna, don't shut me out. You get so quiet when you're mad. I want to share your hurts as well as your joys."

Adrianna nodded and kissed his red-rimmed ear. "I'll start banging on the piano when I'm mad," she said, laughing. "I know now I can let you into my soul and you'll love me, no matter what."

"Lily thinks one reason she and Harrison stay so happy is that they never go to bed angry."

Adrianna laughed. "I may keep you up fighting 'til dawn, but I won't go to sleep without being in our bed and kissing you good-night." She stroked her finger over his straight nose and firm chin. "I've been so afraid that you'd take your love away to punish me like my family does that I've been my own worst enemy, pushing you away when I needed you most. Now I understand the depth of your love, but will you stay in love with me?"

"You bet I will!" Foy grinned at her with a gleam in his eye. "It's a funny thing, but a really caring, Bible-based love keeps the fires of passion aflame."

Soft night sounds rippled round them, filling their glass tower. Silently, they stood watching the surrounding stars, feeling the wonder of being joined by God. Foy whispered a thankful prayer against Adrianna's fragrant hair.

Blissfully, Adrianna murmured, "Fairy tales do come true, but with a little work instead of a magic wand."

Suddenly she stirred in Foy's sheltering arms and asked fearfully, "Oh, dear! What about Lily and Harrison? How will they feel about me?"

"Darling, you've touched their hearts from the beginning. Lily hurt for you because you had never been given love and affection. She wanted to help you find her Savior." He kissed her gently. "And they, of all people, understand about Green."

Green. The thought of him brought them back to the earth. They looked down. Flaming torches showed figures moving on the shore.

"Uh-oh," Foy said. "I almost missed our most important landing." Releasing her, he gave orders into the speaking tube and eased the boat toward shore.

"What? You mean we still have a chance?"

Foy grinned. "We had allowed some time for getting by King's Rock that we didn't have to use. Didn't you notice we stopped a while back?"

"Yes."

"Harrison telegraphed ahead." Suddenly Foy was dancing from one foot to the other in excitement. "Just you wait."

They climbed down from the peaceful isolation of the pilothouse. Adrianna hugged Lily and shared her joy.

"Last night I accepted Jesus as my personal Savior. I thought that I was a Christian because my name was on a church roll and I tried to be morally upright. I didn't know I was lost. I've been searching—but I didn't know what for until you showed me. Thank you, Lily."

"I'm so very happy," replied Lily with tears shining in her eyes. "Keep studying, growing, learning everything you can, but remember: Always let philosophy fit into your faith instead of making faith fit into your philosophy."

"And test any idea by the measure of Christ," Emma added, kissing her cheek.

Silence suddenly shattered. Hammers pounded, boards splintered as workmen stripped the steamer of excess poundage. Spars, doors, windows were carried down the gangplank.

Adrianna, Lily, and Emma pulled their chairs out of the ladies' saloon. Furniture from the main cabin and staterooms was placed on the dock.

One crew marched out removing weight while another boarded, stuffing the *Mignonne*'s hold with fuel. Ratty looking men, lounging about the waterfront, slapped their knees and swapped racing tales as they watched six barrels of rosin being rolled aboard. Their eyes bulged as barrel after barrel of kerosene followed. When huge burlap bundles of fat pine stumps thumped onto the cargo deck, they declared they had never seen such a load of hot fuels.

The bell clanged; the whistle blasted. The last man jumped ashore. The plank lifted. The *Mignonne* pulled swiftly away from the landing. Cheers rose from the crowd as well-wishers waved their arms above their heads.

Black smoke belched from the two tall smokestacks. Cinders fell unnoticed on the women clutching the rail, watching the dark river.

Lily staunchly declared she trusted Harrison's judgment, but Emma remained silent with her lips pressed tightly. Watching Emma's pale face, Adrianna knew she feared for Jonathan who had lost his foot to a boiler explosion.

Unable to remain still, Adrianna ran below to see the engine room for herself. Her eyes widened at the sight of the boiler, glowing red.

Wiping sweat from his dirty face, Jonathan watched the

boiler gauges. Roaring flames leaped from the open doors of the huge furnaces. Two burly men poked the fire with long rods, stirring kerosene-soaked wood. Her nose burning from the fumes, Adrianna stepped back.

Squeezing through a break in the teetering cotton bales, Adrianna crept to the edge of the lower deck. They were traveling far too fast to be safe. Surely there was something she could do to help.

Pulling, tugging, she dragged a bundle of the lightwood knots toward the boiler room. Wordlessly, Lily joined her.

Bam! The *Mignonne* struck solidly, stopped. Scurrying back through the crevice, Adrianna saw the bow was mired in mud.

Clang! The pilot signaled for backing.

They pulled her out. Undamaged, the *Mignonne* steamed on.

Squinting, rubbing her eyes, Adrianna saw the sky was lighter even though rain was falling. "Oh, Lily!" She panted. "Day is coming. What if—after all this—Green's ship doesn't wait until eight o'clock? What if he leaves before dawn?"

"No." Lily laughed ruefully. "He won't do that. One of Green's fatal charms is his sense of honor."

Swish, swish, swissss. The paddle wheel was slowing. The firemen were burning the empty rosin barrels. In their excitement at making a burst of speed, they had used it all. Wood racks were empty. The spluttering gauge was flopping slowly.

The *Mignonne* floated toward shore. The gangplank splashed down, bounced as serious-faced men ran down, shouldered wood, hurried back. No laughter or joking sounded this time. Suddenly a chanting song began, steadying their rhythm.

"Oh, can't they carry more than one piece at a time?"

Adrianna checked her watch and glanced at the grave face of Lily who seemed as determined as she to remain at the center of activity in spite of the rain.

Lily shook her dark hair. "You don't know how heavy cord wood is." She let out a long sigh and pointed to a nattily dressed man sheltered by a big, black umbrella as he paced the dock. "That must be Green's agent. This is our last stop to wood up."

As they pulled back into the stream, the rain became a downpour. The lovely boat seemed to cough tiredly, unable to gain momentum as the rain-soaked wood sputtered, smoked, went out. Kerosene was added liberally, but the fire burned disinterestedly.

Foy clopped down from above. Trusting Mr. Trimmer with the wheel, he joined the boiler-room crew.

"This wood's no good!" Jonathan shouted. "It's water-logged, but—worse—it's not the porous red oak we ordered. If I throw on enough kerosene, it will finally burn, but it will never make a hot fire. It's dead wood!"

"Do you think Green had rotten wood placed there?" Adrianna gasped.

"It's the kind of thing he would do," Lily replied.

Foy's eyebrows knit in a determined scowl. "The kerosene won't last at the rate you're using it. Bring all the li'dard." He grabbed an axe. Muscles rippling beneath his wet white shirt, Foy split the knotted wood into splinters. Adrianna picked up a piece. The pungency of turpentine penetrated her senses. The stumps, like so many oily-backed ducks, yielded tender insides streaked red-gold, dry.

"Reminds me of your hair." Foy winked.

"Not now." She laughed and dabbed at the loose strands clinging wetly to her dirty face.

Family and crew worked, endeavoring to kindle the dead wood with the rosin-rich pine. Each added splinter blazed, elicited a brief glow from the logs, consumed itself, was gone. The supply of fat lightwood was exhausted, yet the smoldering fire refused to burn.

Bedraggled, the whole family stood on the boiler deck and clasped hands.

Foy patted the *Mignonne*'s side as if to tell her goodbye. "I'm sorry. I'll make it up to y'all somehow."

"So near," said Harrison, pointing.

Etched against the streaks of morning lay the skyline of Apalachicola.

"It's almost light." Foy raked his hands through his hair. "Light," he repeated. "Light!" he shouted. "Adrianna, Emma, run! Gather all the candles from the cupboards. I'll get the crates of 'em from the storeroom."

"Lily," said Harrison, catching Foy's excitement. "Take a crew to the kitchen. Bring the slabs of bacon, all the fat sidemeat and grease. We aren't beaten yet!"

Scattering like mice over the huge boat, everyone snatched up combustibles. The candles, flung atop the wood, dripped enflaming wax. Fat meat sizzled, igniting wood. Kitchen grease burst into flames. Resisting no longer, the dead wood leaped into blazing gold and blue, then banked into hot, red coals.

With a mighty belch of fire and smoke, the *Mignonne* shot forward into Apalachicola Bay.

Green flags flying identified a majestic ship riding at anchor on the ocean swells. A signal flag fluttered as they were sighted.

Cheers rang out from the exhausted crew of the *Mignonne*. The family gathered on the upper deck and Harrison offered a prayer of thanks.

Adrianna and Foy leaned eagerly out at the bow, facing joyfully into the wind. Rivers of testing fire lay behind them. Safe in each other's arms, they needed no words. Bracing as the riverboat hit the rough waves of the sparkling, blue-green Gulf, Adrianna breathed salt air. The magnificent vastness of God's creation enraptured her. Times were changing. They were moving out from their small world, but God was out there, too, bigger than the universe, in control of all history.

Foy hugged Adrianna close and nuzzled his face into her brilliant hair. A new day was dawning; beyond the horizon lay a new century. With a sure course charted, they were ready to meet the challenge.

acknowledgments

The steamboat days of the 1870s on the shallow, shoal-ridden Chattahoochee River between Alabama and Georgia were brought to life for me by Edward A. Mueller, author of *Perilous Journeys: A History of Steamboating on the Chattahoochee, Apalachicola, and Flint Rivers, 1828-1928*. Mueller shared his extensive collection of first-hand accounts, many of which were extracted from microfilm of Columbus, Georgia, newspapers by T. J. Peddy.

The boats, excursions, landmarks, and disasters are all true, however I have compressed dates and fictionalized. Mueller helped me make a fictional composite which is as accurate as possible to this particular time and river.

Some of the best articles which I drew from were: *Steaming on the Chattahoochee*, by W.C. Woodall, *Georgia Magazine*, Aug.–Sept. 1969, *Romance Along the Alabama Rivers*, by J.H. Scruggs, Jr., *Weekly Philatelic Gossip*, Sept. 19, 1953, and *River Steamboats Were Way To Go*, edited by Ed Mueller from the Bainbridge, Georgia, newspaper of 1877, printed in the *Tallahassee Democrat*, July 10, 1966.

The *Cannonball Route* was actually set as the fastest schedule on the Chattahoochee in 1886 by the steamer *William D. Ellis* of the People's Line.

The Reconstruction Era came to a close in Eufaula as I have described it with the riot on Lily and Harrison's anniversary. Facts came from "The Eufaula Riot of 1874," by Harry P. Owens, *The Alabama Review*, July, 1963, pp.

224–237. Much other information was gleaned from Anne Kendrick Walker's *Backtracking in Barbour County* (Richmond, 1941).

I would like to thank Fleming H. Revell Publishers for use of material about Darwin in "Cut Out God" from *Tarbell's Teacher's Guide*, 1983–84, p. 247.

Thanks goes to Mimi Rogers, chief curator of the Jekyll Island Museum, for permission to draw from a wedding exhibit, and to P. J. Thomas, manager, Springer Opera House Arts Association, Inc., for information on a play which opened there November 7, 1874.

Douglas Purcell, executive director of the Historic Chattahoochee Commission, searched out information and took me to Fendall Hall which inspired my Barbour Hall. On the National Register of Historic Places, Fendall Hall is preserved as a museum by the state of Alabama. The painting of its parlor and dining room was actually done by Monsieur Le Franc about 1886. This beautiful house is open to the public several days each week through the auspices of RSVP of Eufaula and Barbour County in cooperation with the Alabama Historical Commission.

Florence Foy Strang introduced me to the delightful events of the Volunteer Firemen. Some of the firemen's artifacts are on display at Shorter Mansion where Hilda Sexton has been very helpful. Other details of the Firemanic Tournaments came from microfilm of the May 15, 1886, *Americus Times-Recorder*.

Americus, Georgia, Fire Chief Morris Smith provided helpful information on fire fighting. Mrs. James T. West, Sr., of DeSoto, Georgia, was at one time the only woman east of the Mississippi who was a licensed cotton sampler and weigher and warehouse manager. Her reminiscences gave life to the scenes of cotton fires.

Again thanks goes to: Lake Blackshear Regional Library and especially Harriet Bates who can unearth the most obscure fact; to the Rev. James Eldridge, Hinton Lampley, Marvlyn and Bill Story, Sandra Bowen, Glenda Calhoun, and Ginny Hodges.

Although the background characters and events are true, the main characters and story are fictional.

A Letter To Our Readers

Dear Reader:

In order that we might better contribute to your reading enjoyment, we would appreciate your taking a few minutes to respond to the following questions and return to:

Karen Carroll, Editor
Heartsong Presents
P.O. Box 719
Uhrichsville, Ohio 44683

1. Did you enjoy reading *River of Fire*?
   ❏ Very much. I would like to see more books by this author!
   ❏ Moderately
   ❏ I would have enjoyed it more if

   _____

2. Where did you purchase this book?_____

   _____

3. What influenced your decision to purchase this book?
   ❏ Cover   ❏ Back cover copy
   ❏ Title   ❏ Friends
   ❏ Publicity   ❏ Other _____

4. Please rate the following elements from 1
   (poor) to 10 (superior).
   ❏ Heroine ❏ Plot
   ❏ Hero ❏ Inspirational theme
   ❏ Setting ❏ Secondary characters

5. What settings would you like to see in
   Heartsong Presents Books?

   _____

   _____

6. What are some inspirational themes you
   would like to see treated in future books?

   _____

   _____

7. Would you be interested in reading other
   Heartsong Presents Books?
   ❏ Very interested
   ❏ Moderately interested
   ❏ Not interested

8. Please indicate your age range:
   ❏ Under 18 ❏ 25-34 ❏ 46-55
   ❏ 18-24 ❏ 35-45 ❏ Over 55

Name _____

Occupation _____

Address _____

City_____ State _____ Zip _____

HAVE YOU MISSED ANY OF THESE TITLES?

These additional titles in our Romance Reader series contain two complete romance novels for the price of one. You'll enjoy hours of great inspirational reading. Published at $7.95 each, these titles are available through Heartsong Presents for $3.97 each.

_____ RR2 A MIGHTY FLAME &
A CHANGE OF HEART *by Irene Brand*

_____ RR3 LEXI'S NATURE &
TORI'S MASQUERADE *by Eileen M. Berger*

_____ RR5 SONG OF JOY &
ECHOES OF LOVE *by Elaine Schulte*

_____ RR7 FOR LOVE ALONE &
LOVE'S SWEET PROMISE *by Susan Feldhake*

_____ RR9 SUMMER'S WIND BLOWING &
SPRING WATERS RUSHING *by Susannah Hayden*

_____ RR10 SECOND SPRING &
THE KISS GOODBYE *by Sally Laity*

LOVE A GREAT LOVE STORY?
Introducing Heartsong Presents —
Your Inspirational Book Club

Heartsong Presents Christian romance reader's service will provide you with four never before published romance titles each month! In fact, your books will be mailed to you at the same time advance copies are sent to book reviewers. You'll preview each of these new and unabridged books before they are released to the general public.

These books are filled with the kind of stories you have been longing for—stories of courtship, chivalry, honor, and virtue. Strong characters and riveting plot lines will make you want to read on and on. Romance is not dead, and each of these romantic tales will remind you that Christian faith is still the vital ingredient in an intimate relationship filled with true love and honest devotion.

Sign up today to receive your first set. Send no money now. We'll bill you only $9.97 post-paid with your shipment. Then every month you'll automatically receive the latest four "hot off the press" titles for the same low post-paid price of $9.97. That's a savings of 50% off the $4.95 cover price. When you consider the exaggerated shipping charges of other book clubs, your savings are even greater!

THERE IS NO RISK—you may cancel at any time without obligation. And if you aren't completely satisfied with any selection, return it for an immediate refund.

TO JOIN, just complete the coupon below, mail it today, and get ready for hours of wholesome entertainment every month.

Now you can curl up, relax, and enjoy some great reading full of the warmhearted spirit of romance.